OLD ENOUGH TO KNOW BETTER

CAROLYN FAULKNER

Published by Blushing Books
An Imprint of
ABCD Graphics and Design, Inc.
A Virginia Corporation
977 Seminole Trail #233
Charlottesville, VA 22901

Carolyn Faulkner
Old Enough to Know Better

eBook ISBN: 978-1-64563-584-0
Print ISBN: 978-1-64563-572-7
v1

Prologue

He took her gently over his lap, and despite how careful he always was, she knew it wasn't going to be good. There was always true regret in his tone at times like this, "I hope you know I can only do this because I adore you."

Unable to speak knowing the next few minutes weren't going to be pleasant, and with tears already gathering in her eyes at the anticipation of the coming pain, Cat nodded, hoping that would be enough. It wasn't always with him. He sometimes demanded more than she thought she could give, all in the name of making sure that she was true to herself, and to him.

"And that I wouldn't do this if I didn't think it was best for you," his lips whispered at her temple before kissing it.

Again, she nodded, biting her lip, feeling the way she always did when he had her in this position—naughty and obviously unhappy at having ended up in this position, sort of. She struggled as he brought her pants and panties to her knees, but not too hard, having learned from experience that resisting him too much really wasn't in her best interest.

His big, already warm hand covered almost the entirety of her bottom as it lay there, innocently enough at the time, patting and rubbing slowly.

1

"Do you know how much I love you?" he breathed, his free hand wandering into the mass of her hair as it spilled down her back.

That was enough to send her over the edge. With him not having yet lifted his hand to crack it down onto her bottom, Cat dissolved into tears, reaching blindly back to capture that wandering hand with her own and grip it as the only solid thing in her world. "At least as much as I do you," she sobbed, kissing his knuckles.

Ignoring the tears in his own eyes in favor of what was best for her, he turned to the situation at hand and the lovely, rounded hillocks he'd much rather caress than spank, but his love for her was such that he would always do what he knew was best for her, without hesitation.

Chapter 1

She kept to the back of the gathering, as usual. These people had been her friends for years and yet she still felt somewhat out of place among them, more than ever since she'd lost Clint. He'd been her rudder at social events. Cat allowed herself a small, sad smile. Without Clint, everything seemed flat, even five years later. She'd pretty much given up the idea that that was ever going to change. When they'd said their long goodbyes while holding each other in their magical bed as the disease that ravaged him slowly claimed his body, everything in her world had adopted a varying shade of gray. Nothing had ever truly been right since, and she'd long since given up the idea that it would ever be.

She was dealing, she told her friends. She was dealing the best she could, which apparently wasn't the way they wanted her to. They—a relatively small group of very close friends she'd had since high school, some since grade school—had decided long since that mourning had gone out with the Victorians. Some of them had tried to set her up only months after Clint had passed on, and she had nearly cut them out of her life for that.

Just because they didn't have the kind of deep, abiding love relationship with their significant others that she'd had with Clint didn't mean they shouldn't respect the idea that she was still trying to come to grips with the fact that she'd scattered her heart along with his ashes over the rocks at Otter Cliffs.

Not that she'd ever been the life of the party, even with him standing strong and stalwart at her side. That wasn't her style at all. She was a quiet person, much preferring to be a homebody than the center of anyone's attention but his. Under his loving, benevolently strict gaze, she bloomed. He'd been her backbone when she had none, her ego, her conscience... her confessor. And no one, but no one, would ever, could ever, replace him.

She was a professional widow now. Every time she said that of herself, she remembered how her mother had come to call herself "a widow on a small, fixed income" whenever she spoke to anyone once Daddy had died. Thanks to Clint's almost obsessive financial planning, she wasn't on a small income. The house was paid for and she had a very tidy nest egg that would likely survive her. Not that she had anyone to leave it to.

Children had never been in their plans. They were much too involved with each other and had decided early on in their relationship that neither of them wanted to risk the perfection of what they'd found with each other to add a child to it. And although they would occasionally daydream about what a child of theirs would have been like, neither of them had ever felt they were missing out.

Clint got into the commercial real estate business early. As a matter of fact, he was still in college for his business degree and was always self-employed, although he took side jobs to make ends meet, as they both did. They'd married right out of high school and the two of them worked their butts off at any job they could. There was no hope of getting ahead, at first, only making it through each month. Having met their financial obligations was an excuse to celebrate, cautiously.

But with Clint's natural financial acumen and both of their sheer hard work, they were able to scrimp and save and buy their first property together, then their first house, and they were off and running from there without ever looking back. Cat had wandered a bit, somewhat undecided as to what she might like to do with her life. In the beginning of their time together, she'd taken any job that would get her a stable salary and cover Clint for health and dental insurance, so she'd spent a lot of time at entry level jobs.

But as their own business flourished, they came to a point where they could afford to buy their own insurance and for her to come into the business as a partner. They found that they were living a retired lifestyle at the ripe old age of thirty-four.

They decided they wanted to do what they had been figuring on doing when they actually did retire, and that was to travel. So they installed Clint's neatnik sister in their house to housesit, knowing it would be in good hands, and set off on the occasional relatively long trip—spending a good amount of time in England, as that was one of Cat's favorite places. She was an unabashed Anglophile and dragged Clint from pillar to post, visiting all the places she'd read about, mostly dealing with the Tudor dynasty. They saw the continent, too, and made return trips to Paris and Rome in particular, although London was hands down their favorite. Clint had even toyed with the idea of gifting Cat with a small apartment there, considering how much time was spent over there, but he decided against it. They'd found a gorgeous bed and breakfast they adored, with owners who came to treat them like family, and he didn't want to change that.

And through it all, unlike a lot of other couples who might

have killed each other being together so constantly, it just brought the two of them closer together. They were truly two halves of a whole, each incomplete without the other.

And a large part of that was the fact that Clint always kept a somewhat benevolent, lovingly watchful eye on his wife at all times. He'd known her since she was a small child, and he'd seen the permissive way her parents had raised her. She was an only child, and although she was never truly a brat, she had never been given much in the way of rules or restrictions. In turn, she'd grown up expecting that things in her life would go a certain way and she could get away with doing certain things and no one would ever call her to account, as her parents had not.

Clint had set about disabusing her of that notion from day one of their relationship. She was spoiled, which wasn't her fault, but that wasn't something he could support or encourage. She'd grown up in a three-person family, in a beautiful fourteen-room turn of the century Victorian. He'd grown up on the wrong side of the tracks, in a five-room house with six people in it. Needless to say, their leaner years were much harder on her than they had been on him. He'd grown up on lean and could squeeze a nickel 'til the buffalo pooped.

The first time she'd crossed that boundary while they were married was when she'd blown one of her paychecks on a beautiful dress, which he certainly appreciated on her at the time, when she'd graced him with an impromptu fashion show in their three room apartment not far from where he'd grown up. He'd gotten home from a long day working at job number three just to help them keep body and soul together and, despite all of the whirling and twirling she'd done, showing off her purchase and the beautiful body beneath it, she'd ended up receiving a rather unexpected comeuppance, especially since the money she'd spent should have gone toward the alarmingly past due electricity bill.

Of course, they had pooled their money. Both of their parents had always had joint accounts and they couldn't imagine not sharing everything. But Clint's idea of sharing everything and Cat's had been two very different things at first, and Clint hadn't realized exactly to what extent Cat's upbringing would affect her spending habits. To his credit, he confessed that to Cat when he sat her down, still wearing the gorgeous dress in question, which he found was distracting him from his true intentions.

It was a royal blue confection that brought out the corn-flower blue in her eyes and accented the wavy blonde hair that fell artfully around her shoulders with little to no effort on her part. Her skin leaned toward a paler than was popular shade, but she burned easily and didn't much favor the sun, making her skin that much softer because of it. When he put his hand on her upper arm to guide her in taking a seat on the bed next to him, it was all he could do to concentrate on what he wanted to say, to say nothing of what he knew he had to do. Everything in him wanted to press her back to that pretty crocheted comforter she'd had in her antique cedar hope chest and have his way with her in the manner he knew would plea-sure her the most.

What stopped him was the sight of the envelope that was sitting on his nightstand, containing the electricity bill that they weren't going to be able to pay unless she returned the dress. That white envelope, with its fluorescent pink "past due" stamp on the front was more than enough to steel his resolve and help him remember that he needed to be strong for the both of them, or they were going to sink instead of swim. He gathered her tight against him, asking in a soft voice, "You have the receipt for the dress, right, Cat?"

She wasn't stupid, and he could feel her tense up immedi-ately. "Yes, it's in the bag. Why?" It was impossible not to tense up when she had a good idea what was going to happen, from his demeanor and his question.

Why, oh why, had she let herself be talked into buying that dress? She'd been out with some friends, just window-shopping. They were supposed to be just window-shopping! Clint had let her to go to lunch with them, even though that was stretching their budget pretty tightly. She knew he wasn't going to be going to a nice, sit down restaurant with any of his friends this month—or any month—but he was like that. He always did everything he could to make sure she got to see the girls, knowing it was important to her to keep in contact with the friends she'd had since she was practically a baby, even if he had to sacrifice a little more for her to do it. He loved her more than enough to eat peanut butter and jelly for lunch in order for her to go out with the girls, because it made him happy to see her happy.

She felt the same about him, of course, but he rarely asked, and when he did, it was something much less expensive —like an occasional fishing or hunting trip with the boys. Since they always went to someone else's lodge, and they split the gas and food bills, his outings ended up costing a lot less than hers did overall.

So she'd gone out, and it was wonderful, as always. But lunch was never all it was. They'd had to go to the mall, of course, and she'd seen this dress on sale, in her size, and it looked fabulous on her. Her friends practically wouldn't let her out of the store without buying it. Of the five friends she was closest with, only two of them—Jane and Rhonda—knew the kind of relationship she had with her husband. They knew he disciplined her when he saw fit, and they both gave her the eye as she brought her purchase to the cash wrap desk, as a picture of that blasted electricity bill, which was about the same cost as the dress, flashed in her mind.

But she wanted that dress, dammit! It looked so good on

her, and she hadn't had a new dress in ages! And he was so loving and wonderful and generous to her, how could she possibly complain to him about something frivolous like that, like the need to go out and spend money just because you found the absolute perfect dress at the absolute perfect price? No man was going to understand that, unless he was gay. And there was no question about Clint in that area.

So she'd bought it anyway, and now, here she was, in his arms, but not for the reason she wanted to be in his arms at all. Cat was already crying. His spankings were nothing to sniff at, and she knew that was where this scene was going to end up. She must've known it when she'd written out the check, but she couldn't quite stop herself.

He pressed his face against the side of her head, burying his nose in her hair and breathing deeply in her scent. "I think you know why," he almost whispered, and that was worse. "You know the money in our account was already earmarked for the electric bill. We just had that discussion a couple of nights ago, didn't we?" Clint's finger turned her face toward him as his lips settled ever so slowly over hers then retreated just slightly. "Didn't we?"

She knew he would wait for her response, but not long. "Yes," she sighed on a sob.

Bless him, he didn't ask her why she'd bought it. Somehow, he knew she didn't know the answer herself and would be much less able to give him a satisfactory reason. He kissed her again, then said in his no nonsense tone that was totally at odds with the tender way he was holding her, "Tomorrow, we're going to the mall to return the dress together, and then we're going to Central Maine Power to pay the bill before they turn our lights off, understood?"

He was never angry or nasty or mean with her. He almost never yelled, and if he did, it was very rarely at her and most usually at himself, or a football or hockey team on television that wasn't playing to his specifications. In this situation, when he was going to discipline her, he was almost dichotomously soothing and sensitive.

Cat nodded, not that she really had a choice, tears falling from her chin onto the leg of his jeans.

"But what's going to have to happen in the meantime, my love?" he asked, adjusting his position a little so he sat straighter on the edge of the bed, less toward her, in preparation for what was to come. But he kept his arm around her, steady, not binding. He didn't fear she'd run away from him, but it was more to provide support and remind her that she could lean on him, even when he punished her. He always sought to remind her that the punishments he dished out didn't mean he didn't love her, and he never wanted her to forget that.

She hated saying it, and Clint almost always required it when he remembered and had the time to go through the entire ritual. He felt it was important for the both of them, so he tried to do it as often as possible. Sometimes, though, when it was a quick spanking, he didn't. Like when he just flipped her over his knee in the living room, or made her bend over in the kitchen, or wherever, usually for sassing him or using a word he didn't like, and there seemed to be an endless list of those, as far as she was concerned. She hated to hear him say her whole name, knowing what was coming next was a lecture about ladylike language, to be accompanied by the loud tattoo of his hand cracking painfully against her bare butt.

"We get to snuggle and make love?" she suggested hopefully, blatantly trying to kiss him into distraction.

Clint knew she didn't have far to go with that, but he had to be strong, for her, and he was determined to do so. So he unwrapped those silky arms from around his neck and set her away from him just a bit, trying to adjust himself into a comfortable position which was damned near impossible with a raging hard on pressed against the zipper of his jeans. "None of that tonight, sweetie. You know the rule."

She knew it and didn't like it. No sex after a spanking; that was his rule. He didn't believe in pleasuring her after he'd punished her, thinking it diminished his efforts, somehow, and he could almost never be corrupted about that. He wouldn't even be dissuaded in the morning, either. She'd tried. They wouldn't be able to come together until tomorrow night, and it would drive her absolutely crazy.

Cat's only consolation was that she knew he would be aching at least as badly as she was—maybe even more, although she doubted it. There was always a conflagration when they came together. Like gasoline and a match, they lit up the sky with their loving, always had, always would.

"Answer my question, Cat." This time he wasn't fooling, and she knew she had better do as he asked, or she'd be getting two spankings—one for not answering him in what he considered to be a timely fashion, and one for buying the dress. Two Clint spankings in a row was never a good idea.

But still, making her say it was a torturous thing, and she squirmed, quite physically, as she barely eked the words out, "A spanking."

"Not just 'a' spanking," he corrected immediately, "*your* spanking. I don't bother to spank just anyone, do I?"

"No," she said, her voice small, repeating, because she knew he would require it of her eventually, "my spanking." She couldn't repress a small shiver.

"Good girl. Now," he patted his legs, "over my lap."

He rarely positioned her himself. Clint preferred that she come to him for her chastisement herself, of her own free will, as if physically consenting to it as well as inherently, every single time. Cat had known exactly what she had signed on to well before they'd actually tied the knot. This definitely wasn't something he'd sprung on her on their wedding night. He'd made it very clear from the beginning of their relationship exactly what he expected from her and how he expected her to behave, as well as exactly how he'd correct that behavior, when needed, from the beginning—since before they were engaged. He'd never hesitated to keep her in line, which had always brought amused smiles to her parents' faces, she'd noted.

But it was downright awful to have to put herself over the lap of the person she knew was going to spank her. It was almost painful in and of itself, forget the spanking. Well, almost. His thighs were so big and muscular that they had a thinnish pillow that he kept at hand to put over them for her comfort, so her ribs and hips would have something to cushion them. But then it would move when she climbed on, and there was always a certain amount of adjustments that had to be made that just contributed to her humiliation.

He was tender and gentle but firmly resolved throughout, patient with her endless fussing and futzing until she felt just right. Cat knew she didn't need to be hurting anywhere else but where he was going to be focusing for the next while, so she was a pain in the butt about her position. She also knew that, true to form, she was going to be flailing about like a mad woman, trying to dislodge herself or avoid a swat or twelve, not caring much at the time which it was. So she needed to be sure she was going to be comfortable the whole time, which seemed like decades at the time, but she was sure it lasted only minutes... but maybe years?

She'd never been cognizant enough at the end to try to keep track. But it wasn't as if Clint beat her to a bloody pulp, either. Far from it. He was always very attuned to how she was responding to what he was doing and very careful not to overdo it. He wasn't a huge man, not a lot taller than she was, but he was definitely much more muscular. And she had to give it to him, he was always scrupulously careful of her when she was in his arms or over his lap.

Her spankings weren't horrible, long, drawn out, torturous affairs, although they certainly seemed as though they were at the time, and she reacted as though they were, crying and kicking as if he was digging her heart out with a spoon. Clint made sure she regretted what she'd done; however long that took, and how harsh the punishment was entirely his decision. She always ended up with a bottom that was sore for several days later, not that he ever hesitated to scorch it again the next day, if he deemed she needed it, darn him.

Clint leaned over to brush her hair back from her eyes and give her a pillow that she could cry into. At that point, they were still living in an apartment building with tissue thin walls. One of their fellow tenants had already banged on the shared wall during a particularly loud punishment session, and Cat had been holding her breath ever since, waiting for the police to arrive on their doorstep.

"I love you, Cat," he said solemnly, for this was not something he ever undertook lightly, and she knew it.

"I love you, too, 'n I'm sorry," she sobbed, and it damned near broke his heart every time, the trust she placed in him and the love she had for him when she let him do this for her.

Chapter 2

When he was through, her bottom radiated a palpable heat that he knew must have been terribly uncomfortable. His handprint was seared all over the length of her rear and the backs of her thighs, which he always deemed needed attention, as he knew they were at least as sensitive as her bottom, if not more. Cat had taken it well, though, even though she'd been crying from before she had even placed herself over his lap. She'd done her best to try to dislodge herself and scoot out from under his well-placed swats but hadn't managed to miss very many.

For a relatively non-athletic woman, she became a world-class contortionist when he had her over his lap, twisting and twirling and writhing and turning herself into a pretzel, trying to avoid any spank she could, and flailing her legs like she should have tried out for Riverdance.

But one well-placed leg over hers quieted that—as soon as he remembered to do it—and the broad arm that usually encircled her waist tightened until she could barely move an inch. That rendered her entirely vulnerable to whatever form of correction he saw fit, without having to worry about being concussed into unconsciousness in the process by the whirling dervish that was his wife.

He never yelled at her for trying to avoid being spanked. He'd been spanked himself when he was growing up—unlike Cat—and he knew that it was darned near impossible not to try to avoid the discomfort it caused. He simply set about, calmly and with excruciating care for her, neutralizing each attempt so that she ended up getting exactly the spanking he intended for her, regardless of her efforts to avoid exactly that end.

Cat was still sobbing quietly into the pillow he'd given her that, luckily, was a spare. She'd drenched it and wouldn't want to sleep on it tonight.

Clint sighed, wanting to rub his hand over the havoc he'd created on her bottom, wanting to rub lotion on it, to soothe away the hurt he'd just deliberately caused. But he restrained himself, knowing she needed the reminder of rolling over onto a sore bottom tonight, and sitting on it tomorrow morning at breakfast, and in the car on the way to the mall when they returned the dress together.

So after divesting her of the dress, which he laid carefully over the chair next to the bed, and popping her into her favorite nightgown, he tried to content himself with being a replacement for the pillow, tugging it away from her and transferring her limp body into his waiting arms as they cuddled close together under the warm covers.

She glommed onto him as she often did after a spanking, as if he was a rock in the middle of a storm, still hiccoughing sobs. He enveloped her in his strong arms and rocked just a bit, back and forth, rubbing her back and just letting her cry it out. Clint loved the feel of her body pressed up against his, and he did all he could to not lay her back and make love to her like every inch of him wanted desperately to. His desire for her hadn't diminished one iota from the moment he'd seen her. If anything, the more time they spent together, the more it grew. The better he knew her, the more intimacies they shared, the more the raging inferno of his desire was stoked.

And just after a spanking was one of the times he desired the deepest intimacies with her the most, yet he had made a rule for her that affected the both of them—and although he knew she probably didn't see it much that way, most all of her rules did affect them both, in one way or the other—and denied himself that ultimate pleasure. He had never broken that rule. Until now.

Clint lifted her face from his shoulder with a finger under her chin, covering her lips with his immediately, insistently.

Cat's mouth was moist and soft. He could feel that their lips were damming what remained of her tears until he rolled with her, tucking her beneath him, insinuating himself between her legs. She gasped and arched her back at the way he took her, all at once, to the hilt, no words, no explanations… simple possession, in its basest of forms.

She was so tight around him, he could feel her body pulsing and trying to accommodate him, her hips arching and rocking as she came to grips with the sudden, stark pleasure of being both pinned and pricked so unexpectedly.

He hadn't so much as moved, beyond claiming her inside and out, and yet she was soaking wet and panting already. Clint reached down and tugged the nightie over her head, hating even the flimsiest of obstacles to the joining of their flesh, top to toe.

Tongues danced, lips sucked, nipples pinched and tweaked

on both sides, and then he reached under her and clenched that still sore, cute little rear of hers that he'd so recently tended to, forcing her even closer against him to avoid his grasping hands, making her groan in a way that had him wishing they were on an island of their own, where no one would ever hear her scream, in pleasure or in pain.

In lieu of the island, he covered her mouth with his and dragged himself out of her so slowly that she was begging him to take her before his hips had made it halfway back.

Her answer was his most evil chuckle, which, to her, was false advertising. There wasn't an evil bone in his body… She thought. But apparently, there was at least one.

Their lovemaking that night was her undoing. In the aftermath, she shook and cried in his arms to the point he thought he might have seriously hurt her, but the truth was far from it. He split her open, the very insides of her, places she never showed anyone. He brought the light of his love to places she didn't even know she owned, and although it was a tender, joyous thing, it wasn't easy, which made it all that much more achingly tender to her.

She fell asleep, as she nearly always did, with her head on his chest and her body throbbing in time to his pulse.

So there she stood, at the very back end of the engagement party for a dear friend, years later, Clintless, alone by choice. She wished she was anywhere else and was thinking too much about old times with a man she'd never see again, who'd never again hold her in his arms or even sear her flesh with his palm. Hell, she'd even gladly sign up for a spanking again without so much as a second thought, if only to be near him.

Tears flooded her eyes, and she turned, wanting to run

home when she knew she should have been trying to enjoy herself at Jane's party. After all, Jane was one of her oldest friends, and she'd been alone, too, raising her first husband's son from his first marriage, Finn, for more than twenty years. Jane's husband had died, too. You would have thought she would have understood better than anyone else what Cat was going through.

But Cat and Clint's relationship wasn't the norm, and neither had Jane and Paul's been. It hadn't been the happiest of marriages, even at its best. Paul's favorite companion had been the bottle, and he'd preferred to take out his shortcomings on Jane, so she actually had less of an understanding of Cat's reluctance to date and come out of mourning than her other friends did.

It was funny. Out of her close friends, there was only one couple that she thought actually had a good relationship, anything like what she and Clint shared. Everyone else had cycled through good and bad relationships like the seasons of the year, picking up and then discarding them for one reason or the other, four out of the five of them ending up alone and seemingly content that way. Three out of four now, she corrected herself, mentally raising her glass to Jane and whatshisname. What was that guy's name? She couldn't come up with it for the life of her. Early Alzheimer's was definitely setting in.

Cat was shaking her head at the way she was slowly losing her mind as she headed for the dining room, where all of the potluck dishes had been laid out for everyone to help themselves. They were spread from hell to breakfast on the groaning, gorgeous mahogany trestle table that had been in Jane's family for more than two hundred years, on the immaculate sideboard that her great-great-great-great grandmother had brought over from the old country with her, and on the

Hoosier that Cat had always not so secretly coveted. Leave it to Jane to have a party for herself and then make everyone else contribute toward it. If it had been Carol's party, she would have had it at the Bar Harbor Inn and she would have spared no expense. Cristal would have flowed like water, and there would have been a huge spread of lobster and caviar and Kobe beef fit for a sheik.

But Jane was much more the down to earth type. They had all been born and bred on the Island, but Jane had retained that down home practicality that some of them had lost. She had inherited a perfectly gorgeous old center hall colonial from her parents, circa 1825, decorated with lovingly treasured antiques that had been handed down from generation to generation, so she didn't feel the need to have her party anywhere else but her own home. Besides, she knew some of her friends were the best cooks in town. Why let that go to waste?

And she was right. Cat took one—and only one, she told herself sternly—of Carol's famous stuffed shells, two paper thin slices of Rhonda's famous garlic studded leg of lamb, a homemade roll that she knew by the cloverleaf shape was Mrs. Kellerman's, and a small—all right, a slab—of Jane's chocolate cheesecake and made her escape to the screened porch, where she was relieved to find no one was at this time of year, to devour her bounty in relative peace and privacy.

It was still a little too chilly for most folks, but the Taylors had gotten a prime piece of land in Southwest Harbor sometime near its inception in 1761, right on the water, back when that didn't mean anything like what it did now in terms of value, and the town was just a small, working fishing village.

She took a slow, calming breath. Even with all her traveling, Cat had never lost her deep love of the smell of the Maine ocean, even at low tide.

CAROLYN FAULKNER

She was just sitting back, having kicked off an uncomfortable high-heeled shoe to place a foot on the cold floorboards, in favor of rocking the swing a little as she listened to the ocean and began to tuck miniscule bite by miniscule bite, into the luscious cheesecake. She started on that first, of course, in case there was an earthquake and the house fell into the sea and she'd started with the roll and missed out for eternity on her last possible bite of chocolate cheesecake, when she heard the screen door open and Finn appeared.

Oh, God, now she had to feel guilty about what she was eating, because someone had caught her. The rule was that if no one saw you eat it, there were no calories, right?

"I thought I'd seen you come out here," he said.

My, my. When did he get old enough to possess a voice like that? It was at least as smooth and guilt inducing as the cheesecake that was melting in her mouth. She cocked her head to one side, thinking that was a relatively strange thing for him to say, too. Why on Earth would he be paying attention to where she was? "I was just trying to escape the crowd, and this has always been my favorite place in this house."

"Mine, too," he said, leaning against the railing of the porch, watching her thoughtfully but in a manner that was making her nervous, nonetheless.

Despite the smooth richness of the dessert, she was beginning to regret that she hadn't brought anything but lemonade out to drink. It really didn't go with cheesecake, and she frowned as she took a sip. It completely ruined the effect.

"Can I get you something else to drink?"

Her eyebrows rose. Wow, an attentive young man, what a novelty. She thought about making the comment out loud but didn't want to offend him. She decided to keep her negative thoughts about the rude, self-absorbed younger generation to herself, since he was one of them.

"Only if you're going to get something yourself."

He levered away from the rail. "What would you like? Champagne? Wine? A cocktail?"

She surprised him by wrinkling her nose and answering, "A big glass of milk? Do you think your mom might have some in the fridge?"

Finn chuckled. "I know she does. She's still trying to get me to drink it, like I'm seven or something. I'll be right back."

Well, he definitely wasn't seven, Cat thought, watching him leave almost absently but letting her eyes dwell where they shouldn't. He had a nice butt that was encased in tight jeans. A very nice butt in very tight jeans. And, if she was pressed to admit it, he had a very nice front, too, a nice package, she believed they called it nowadays. She wasn't much for noticing the physicality of any one—male or female. She became attracted to personality traits primarily, intelligence being first and foremost. But she had to admit, he was quite an attractive young man. Too young for her, of course, but still. She could appreciate the eye candy. She was older, yes, but not dead. Yet.

It was a surprising thing for her, though. She didn't usually notice men, or rather, she hadn't since Clint had died. Frankly, she hadn't much when she was with Clint; there hadn't been any need. She'd had found the perfect man. Why look around when the ultimate in perfection slept next to you each night?

He was back before she knew it, handing her a big red plastic cup which she drained a third of on the first gulp. It tasted luscious mixed with all of that velvety chocolate goodness. "Thank you. Lemonade and cheesecake don't mix."

"Bleh," he shuddered. "No."

"Do you mind if I eat?" she asked, raising her plate toward him. "You're welcome to have some, if you'd like," she offered, greedily hoping he wouldn't take her up on it.

"No, thanks, go right ahead. Mom's been feeding me so much since I came home that I'm going to have to buy a whole new wardrobe twelve sizes up." He patted an entirely nonexistent belly.

Cat snorted very unsympathetically and tried to delicately shovel another piece of cheesecake into her mouth, then gave up trying to be delicate. Who was she trying to impress, anyway? She would've bet anything he had washboard abs under that dress shirt and casually unbuttoned jacket, and she could hardly pretend to match them. "Puh-leeze."

"She is! You know how she cooks."

Cat nodded vehemently. Jane had grown up in a large family, and she cooked like a dream, but enough for an army, even though it had really only ever been herself and Finn. She and Clint had been on the receiving end of Jane's charity overflow and had been extremely grateful at the time when she'd gone on a baking or cooking or canning binge.

"You're no slouch in that department, either, as I remember," he added.

She nodded her head back and forth, saying, "I can hold my own in a kitchen, but I'm nothing compared to your mom in the way of quantity." Finished, and delicately licking her lips, she set the plate aside on a wicker end table. "So you came back here from Silicon Valley? Your mom was really surprised that you'd moved back. She figured you were out there for good. Weren't you happy out there, where it never rains and there's no snow or mud season?"

He chuckled softly and shouldered himself away from the wall to join her on the swing. It was an average sized porch swing that suddenly had Cat feeling very crowded. Trying not to let him see quite how uncomfortable she was at his proximity, she turned toward him to talk, her back against the arm rest, one arm along the back of the swing.

When he sat down, he took over the swinging motion for her, for which she was just as happy; her foot was so cold, it was about to fall off. But before she could tuck the nearly blue appendage under her to warm it up, he'd claimed it and brought it all the way from the floor onto his lap.

"Jeez, your foot must be frozen! It's not very warm out here to be barefoot." Now that sounded uncomfortably like something Clint would say, just before he made her put her shoe back on. Finn began to rub her foot briskly, then he massaged it absently while he answered her question. "Oh, I did what I wanted to do out there, so now I'm home."

"And what was that?" She knew she should have reclaimed her foot as soon as he'd taken possession of it, but his big, warm hands felt wonderful on it, and it had been so long since anyone had rubbed her feet…

Cat wished he hadn't mentioned how cold it was on the porch, because now she was getting cold overall, not just her foot. She folded her arms across her chest, trying to warm herself up.

While he was speaking, he gave her back her foot suddenly, stood up, and draped his jacket over her. "Make a lot of money." He didn't sound like he was trying to brag, and she knew from Jane's accounts that her stepson, whom she considered to be her own as much as if she'd birthed him herself, was now filthy rich from having developed something that had to do with websites communicating with each other. Neither of them understood it much further than that.

Cat was much more distracted by his gallant gesture than by his statement, although that would eventually hit her, too. She was immediately enveloped and surrounded by the latent heat and smell of him, and he smelled like what he was—a young, vital male who wore a faint but slightly spicy after-shave. He was bigger than Clint was by a long shot—taller and broader and more muscular.

She fairly drowned in the fabric of his coat, surrounded by the very essence of him, as well as that primeval warmth. She should have returned the jacket to him immediately, just on general principles, but she couldn't quite bring herself to do it. It felt too good, frankly, to be so warm and yet still smell the sharp salt air. And him.

Yet a loud, insistent voice within her cried out at how wrong it was—that he wasn't Clint, and she was betraying him, just by accepting another man's kindness. And his foot massage. There was definitely going to be guilt enough to go around about that, too, when she took the time to think about it.

"In a nutshell, I created something that made it easier for business computers to talk to each other and exchange credit card information. It simplified the back end of online purchasing for businesses, and it was very simple to use and understand, and it took off." He shrugged as he settled back down after stealing a bit of what was left of her roll and a bit of butter to slather on it. His sigh when he bit into it was akin to sexual. He closed his eyes and his head lolled back as he groaned, "I hope old Mrs. Kellerman has taught someone else in that family how to make these rolls!"

She chuckled at his sheer, unadulterated bliss but somewhere inside her was somewhat alarmed at the idea that no one of her generation called Mrs. Kellerman "old Mrs. Kellerman." Granted, Finn wasn't that much younger than she was. Jane's husband had been older than she was, and Finn was only ten or so years younger.

But still, it was an uncomfortable reminder of the differences between the two of them, enough of one that Cat rose and slid out from under the protective heat of his jacket. He opened one eye, looking up at her suspiciously. "Leaving so soon? Was it the Mrs. Kellerman inspired orgasmic groan? I can imagine how you'd find that squicky. Or the fact that I stole your last piece of roll?" But he still munched down the last bit unrepentantly, as if worried she might try to reclaim it from him in a fit of pique.

Cat found herself staring down into unbelievably deep, brown eyes that were fringed with the thickest, darkest black lashes she'd ever seen. Lashes like that were wasted on a man, she thought incongruously. And he was a man, dammit, no longer the boy she'd watched grow up. She couldn't help but smile, though. He was too damned handsome for his own— and definitely her—good, and he had always seemed to be in a good mood no matter what was going on. In that, he reminded her of Clint, and that was enough to pull her back from her addled, schoolgirl musings about a boy who was entirely too young for her, to say nothing of the fact that he was the son of one of her best friends.

She hadn't been thinking of him that way, had she, really? The thought was a disturbing one, and she latched onto it without even thinking of answering his teasing question. Instead, she stepped back into her shoe, gathered up her plate, gave the place a quick scan to make sure she hadn't missed anything and headed back into the house. Abrupt, yeah. Rude, probably. Absolutely necessary for her mental health? Hell, yes.

Jane wasn't hard to find; Cat could hear her cackling laugh above the thick Maine accents and the occasional French Canadian patois in the front parlor. She did her best to avoid this room for its floor to ceiling, four walled Rogues' Gallery that was rife with pictures of friends and family, which naturally included several of herself and Clint. She threw her plate away, put the milk back that Finn had probably left out, and took a deep breath, knowing she was going to have to convince Jane that she wasn't ducking out of the party early just to go home and sulk.

But Jane was surprisingly easy to convince, only because she was sitting on her new fiancé, Ted's, lap, and she was at least two sheets to the wind and much more interested in French kissing Ted than worrying about whether or not Cat was mooning over her dead husband. Cat, for one, was glad to see that her friend was having a good time and was truly happy, and also that she wasn't going to have to go through the third degree just to get to her car, and that it was easy to concentrate on Jane's adolescent antics and she could forget all the pictures around her of herself and her wonderful husband during much happier times.

Chapter 3

S lipping away carefully, she hadn't expected to run into him again, but there he was, standing by the front door as if he'd appointed himself the doorman, or as if he was waiting for her, she thought fleetingly, dismissing the idea immediately as ridiculous.

"Have you had anything to drink, Catherine? Do you need a ride home?" he asked solicitously, although she sensed an underlying note in his tone that she refused to acknowledge, preferring, instead, to fly by him with a fake smile plastered on her face.

"No, thank you, I rarely drink anymore." She flashed him what she hoped was a sufficiently pleasant smile, wrapped her coat around herself, and ducked out the door. She knew she should have exchanged more pleasantries, that she was acting like an idiot in just needing to get out of that place, and frankly, to get away from a young man who hadn't said or done anything that wasn't simply kind and thoughtful toward her. But he'd put her on edge, somehow, made her aware of herself in a way she hadn't been in a while, and she didn't like it. Not at all. Nope. Didn't like it. Not in the least. Not her.

She refused to examine why her heart was beating so quickly, and her palms—and other areas of her person—were growing moist, and she was panting slightly. But she definitely didn't like the way he made her feel. Definitely.

It was strange to hear him call her by her first name. Her friends were relatively strict, old-fashioned parents, and their children never called their parents' friends by their first names, ever. She had been Mrs. Taylor to Finn, until the day she'd seen him off to college with Jane and the few times she'd seen him when he'd come home since then. Cat wondered how she'd suddenly been promoted—or was she being downgraded —to Catherine?

And no one ever called her Catherine, except for Clint, and only very occasionally, when he was very unhappy with her. And then, he'd usually used it in conjunction with the rest of her full name and that particular tone that, even just remembering, gave her butterflies in her stomach, as in, "Catherine Angelique Taylor, I want to see you front and center in the bedroom, right now." Still, he never yelled it, but that was almost worse.

As she got into her black cherry Nissan 370Z—one of her very few indulgences since Clint had died—she could see that Finn was still standing in the doorway, watching her. She managed a small wave as she backed out but laid a little rubber heading toward her sanctuary—the house they'd bought clear on the other side of the Island.

It was a smallish place that did nothing to reflect their net worth, but then, they didn't need to flaunt what they had. They had only to make themselves comfortable, and since they didn't have anyone else—including children or grandchildren —to consider, they got exactly what they wanted. It was a two-bedroom house that their realtor, at the time, told them would be hard to resell, but neither of them was looking at it for the resale value. They wanted a place on the Island that they could call their own, and although they could have afforded to have built a house of their own design, Cat loved the flavor and character of the older houses that had been built around the turn of the century or even earlier.

The place they'd found was smaller than it might have been, considering that families during that timeframe were necessarily larger. It had been lovingly restored by a professional, who had also been married, with no children, to a wife who loved to cook and entertain. So the master bedroom was a gorgeous suite, with a bathroom and dressing room/closet area, the kitchen had the latest in appliances, including dual wall ovens, stainless steel appliances and mauve granite countertops, and the living room was a warm room, with gorgeous wood floors, a skylight and, for those cold Maine winters, a Franklin stove tucked into one corner that would heat them right out of the house and into the Bangor Mall some days.

They weren't well off enough to be able to afford what they really would have liked, which was to have a huge chunk of land well away from everyone else, right on a nice sandy beach that faced open ocean. There wasn't much sandy beach to be had on the Island, indeed, in northern Maine at all. That was the province of the southern coast of the state. But the house wasn't far from the mouth of a large inlet, with a big, screened porch off the living room and decks off the master bedroom and kitchen that faced the river. They breakfasted with the tides every morning through the early spring and as late into the fall as Clint would allow her to sit out there, shivering happily and eating her bagel.

They had water access, with their small boat tied to a tidy dock for exploring at the spur of the moment, tide permitting, and Cat couldn't count the hours she'd spent hunting for treasures along the shore—sand dollars and dimes, sea glass, and shells with which to fill the house. Whenever she came back with a basketful, Clint always suggested he was going to have to move out to make room for them, which only earned him a withering glance from his long suffering wife. The fact that he was potentially right was beside the point.

Cat drove right into the right bay of the two car garage she'd insisted they add on first thing, although Clint had bellowed loudly about it at first, like a wounded moose, clutching his dwindling wallet as if it had received a mortal blow. But the first snow of winter that year, which if she recalled correctly, had been about eighteen inches, when they didn't have to slog out to unbury the cars and then move them for the plow and then move them again so they didn't get tick- eted—or worse, booted and then towed—because of the town's plowing efforts, she never let him forget just whose genius idea it had been, despite the cost, which wasn't anything to sniff at.

She would never get used to just how quiet the place was when she got home. No Sports Center blaring, no one yelling at a player to run or skate or throw or whatever faster. No mess in the kitchen to deal with, even. She'd gladly clean up every bit of his mess…

She dropped her purse on the big oak hutch in the entryway of the kitchen and consciously reeled in her thoughts. That way led nowhere. Bargaining never worked and only left her feeling even more morose. The whole time he'd been dying, he'd never worried about himself. He'd always said it was the devil who needed to worry, since he was going to take over once he got down there. Clint worried about her—that she would do exactly what she was doing, what she tried desperately, for his sake, not to do—wallow in the loss of him and crawl right into the grave after him.

He made her promise that after she'd taken some time to mourn, she'd get herself together and live the rest of her life as if he was there. Do fun stuff, and yes, even find someone else. The first time he'd mentioned that idea, she'd gotten so mad, she'd nearly struck him. That had never happened in the history of their relationship, but it was a concept, especially in that situation, that she simply couldn't countenance.

As always, he'd understood. And he just kept telling her, occasionally, when she least expected it, that it was okay for her to live the rest of her life to its fullest. That was what he wanted her to do, that it would only honor him and his memory if she did so.

The schlub. Sometimes she hated him for being so goddamn noble. She knew she wouldn't have been anywhere near as wonderful as he had been if their roles had been reversed, and she would have been a complete shrew about the idea of him finding someone else after she was gone, damn him.

She, the sports hater, turned on Sports Center and grabbed the ever present pint of Ben and Jerry's Karamel Sutra from the freezer in one hand, a spray bottle of whipped cream tucked under her arm, and a big serving spoon in the other and headed for his recliner. It still smelled of him, years later, and it was where she went when she missed him the most. Ben and Jerry helped some, but being surrounded by his scent helped the most. It was almost as if he was there, with her, holding her.

Luckily, there wasn't much of the pint left, although she did kill her cholesterol level by finishing off the can of what passed for whipped cream by spraying it into her mouth very unrepentantly. Might as well give the Lipitor something to work on, she thought as the can began to sputter and empty.

The big king-sized bed was much too empty, but then again, she turned on the television and it helped, as it always had for her. She found old episodes of Roseanne on Nick at

Nite and fell asleep to them, much later than she'd intended, due to the sugar rush.

A man with impossibly deep brown eyes was hovering over her. She was nude, at home, in her own bed, and she was never nude there anymore, although she couldn't really remember why just then. He was distracting her too much, talking to her while he was walking, almost parading around in front of her in too tight jeans and a tight black t-shirt.

"I can give you a ride, Mrs. Taylor, if you need one. Do you need one?

The way he posed the question let her know that it wasn't a car ride he was offering. And she needed one. Badly. No, she didn't, her mind and conscience screamed indignantly, but much too late to catch her body that was several lengths ahead of them.

Then he hunkered down, right in front of where she was lying on the bed, not touching her. He wouldn't dare touch her. Clint would... Clint would what? Clint couldn't help her anymore, she remembered. *No, he can't. Clint can't help you anymore. But you don't need help, Catherine. You need this.*

He never stopped looking right into her eyes. He never looked anywhere else the whole time, even when he reached right out and claimed her breast with his big hand, as if it was his God given right to do so, covering the entirety of it and smiling broadly when he felt that taut tip straining against his palm.

No, no, her nipple should not be peaking. It shouldn't. *Stop that, right now!* Her body was about as obedient to her as she had been to Clint sometimes, which wasn't at all.

And he was still smiling beatifically down at her as his other hand landed on the foot it had so wonderfully massaged last night and trailed possessively up from there, tickling the back of her knee, the insides of her thighs, and then tucking itself between her legs to cup the hot moistness of her.

She should have been fighting him. She should have been screaming bloody murder. No one should be touching her there but her husband, Clint.

One thick, strong finger made its way between those soft wet lips, forging ahead into the wet depths of her. He leaned down, still touching her nowhere else but her breast and her pussy, whispering, "If you didn't want me, I wouldn't be here, Catherine. It's your dream."

And then the tip, just the barest tip of that callused finger, slid firmly over her eager swollen clit. She couldn't pry her eyes away from his. He required that she look at him and she couldn't look away, even though she desperately wanted to.

He was different from Clint, stricter in a different way, and she was responding to him even though she didn't want to. Her body was betraying her with him, primed and ready. The evidence was drenching his hand, and achingly peaked between his fingertips as he pinched and gently twisted her nipple.

His fingers never stopped teasing her as he said, "I want you to come, Catherine. You must obey me in this, or I will spank your bottom 'til you can't sit down for a week."

Much to her deep shame and distress, just the merest thought of being spanked by him—by a man who was so much younger than she was—sent her right over the edge, had her contracting immediately, harder than she had in years...

The phone blaring next to her was what woke her the next morning. Without opening her eyes, she brailed her way to it, still contracting, hit the talk button, and said in a distinctly unwelcoming tone, "Go away."

"And a pleasant good morning to you, too, sunshine!"

"Bite me. What the hell are you calling me at the crack of," she barely opened one eye, then closed it immediately, "nine for?"

Unfortunately, Jane remained entirely unfazed by Cat's lack of a warm reception. Sometimes really good friends could be a royal pain in the ass. "I just wanted your thoughts about how the party went last night."

Cat cleared her throat, desperately wishing she couldn't remember the dream she was having before she'd been so rudely awakened, but she was disturbed to realize that it was as fresh in her mind as if she'd actually lived the experience this morning. "Shouldn't you be hung over?" She couldn't keep the note of hope from her voice. If Jane was hung over, maybe this would be a short phone call. It was a false hope, though. Short phone calls weren't much in Jane's repertoire.

Jane snorted. "I know enough to drink a big glass of water before I go to bed. What do you think I am, an amateur?"

"I think you enjoyed your own party, which is exactly what's supposed to happen." She yawned loudly, not bothering to cover the receiver.

"Jeez, did I wake you?"

"Yes, you did, as a matter of fact." If her sex dream had been about anyone else, she might have mentioned it to Jane as a reason for not being so happy to have been awakened, but she wasn't about to go there with the mother of the man who had starred in that highly erotic, but entirely inappropriate, dream.

"Well, then you'd better get up 'cause I sent Finn over a few minutes ago to return your casserole dish."

Cat sat bolt upright in the bed, now wide awake. "You what? Why? It's not like it's Royal Doulton or anything, you know."

"Yeah, but I know it's one of your good dishes—the Johnson Brother's pattern that Clint got you. I remembered and I knew you'd want it back as soon as possible."

That really was a sweet thing for Jane to have done, but couldn't she have just brought it over herself instead of sending Finn over, like he was an eight year old, to do her errands? "Thank you." She got up and began to dress immediately.

"I didn't see you much during the party. Did you have a good time?"

What the hell was she going to put on? She was staring at a closet full of clothes, none of which she wanted to wear to face a man she'd just had a sex dream about. "Yes, I definitely did. It was a great turn out, and I'm so happy that you've finally found someone who makes you happy. Ted's a very lucky man."

She hoped she'd thrown enough platitudes in there to make Jane's ear catch on something that would keep her from asking another question, so she could worry about what to wear and what condition the house was in.

Jackpot. "Oh, I think I'm the lucky one," Jane preened. "Ted is so…" She wandered off into a glowing description of Ted and his attributes—mental, emotional and physical—in such detail that Cat cringed to hear out of the corner of her ear. But it allowed her to decide that she would be damned if she was going to dress up for any kid, even if he was more than halfway to gorgeous and she was still moist from having had a wet dream about him.

Hell, she almost never dreamt about Clint. And she never dreamt about her mom or dad, or any of her friends. But there he was, Finn, her best friend's stepson, larger than life, bringing her off like he did it every night, for crying out loud.

Just about the time she'd hung up the phone with Jane, who was still really waxing poetic about her new love, and had climbed into a pair of pink sweats and an ancient T-shirt that said, "Good Girls Just Never Get Caught," that Clint gave her

35

for Christmas one year, thinking it was absolutely hilarious, when the doorbell rang.

She hadn't had breakfast yet, had no makeup on, and she didn't think she'd even brushed her teeth, but she opened the door anyway. After all, he was only the son of a good, old friend, returning a dish from a party last night that they had all three attended—his mother's—one of her oldest and dearest friend's engagement party.

"Hi, come on in," Cat offered, determined to keep things on an even, casual level.

He seemed surprised that she was so cordial. "I hope I'm not waking you…" He trailed off, looking around the house apologetically.

"Oh, no, your mom already did that for you." Cat took the dish from him and put it in the cupboard. Jane, organized, as usual, had already washed it. "Can I get you some coffee or something?" It wasn't morning without a good, strong cup of coffee, as far as she was concerned. Something that would scrape the varnish right off your insides, melt the spoon and the cup and the table beneath it, preferably.

"Please. Mom's off caffeine since Ted's got heart problems."

"Oh, dear, I wasn't aware of that."

"Yeah. I've been having to go out to get a decent cup of coffee, but as I remember it, yours always was the best."

She couldn't help it, she preened under his compliment. "Aw, thank you. I just make it like my dad liked it—like paint thinner. Probably fit to be condemned by the FDA, but it'll keep you going until the next one." She set the automatic drip machine going, then folded her arms over her chest awkwardly when she realized that he had been watching her intently.

"So how long are you back for?" Cat asked, grasping for conversation. Then she remembered that she had some left-over sausage and egg breakfast casserole in the fridge from the last time she'd had the girls over for brunch and offered him some.

"Oh, yes, please. You know Mom doesn't do anything that has to do with eggs, and that looks great."

She cut a slab for him and a much smaller one for herself, doctored them each a bit with some fresh herbs and cheese to perk them up, then nuked them separately, since she'd gotten a smaller microwave, as it was just the one of her now.

"Juice? I hesitate to offer it, but milk? I also have fresh squeezed grapefruit juice, believe it or not. It's much sweeter than you might think, and only slightly pulpy."

His face brightened. "I remember you used to have that all the time when I hung around here a couple of summers ago because Mr. Taylor—Clint—preferred it to orange juice, right?"

"Yes, yes, he did, and I've come to prefer it, too."

"That sounds great."

Cat had forgotten that Finn and Clint had grown close for several summers while Finn was growing up. They'd rented a house not far from Jane's, and Finn had spent a lot of time with Clint in the garage, helping him fix up an old car he'd bought for just that purpose. They'd always had their heads together whenever she brought out coffee for Clint and milk for Finn. She knew Clint had enjoyed the experience enormously, not having had a son himself to pass his knowledge onto; he was able to do so with Finn.

When they finally settled down to share a breakfast, it was somewhat awkward for Cat. Literally, the only person who had ever sat across from her at their little breakfast bar was Clint. But now, here was this strapping man who dwarfed her and the seat he was perched somewhat gingerly on, literally devouring the huge slab of casserole she'd given him.

She had barely taken two bites of hers before she was up and whisking his plate away from him, offering him more.

Finn hesitated. "I don't want to eat you out of house and home."

But Cat laughed. "It's nice to have someone to eat with, and it'll just go to waste otherwise. I overcooked the last time we had a girls' Sunday brunch, so you might as well have as much as you want."

He nodded, and she gave him round two.

Cat watched him eat that just as voraciously as the first slab and shook her head, smiling. "No wonder your mom was always crying about the grocery bills!"

He had the good grace to blush deeply. "I know. I was just a growing boy then, and I don't have that excuse anymore. I've gotta stop eating like that. I'm not twenty anymore."

She poured the both of them more juice and ventured a question that she wasn't at all sure she wanted to know the answer to. "How old are you now? I've lost track."

"I'll be thirty four in October," he stated seriously, looking at her intently, like he was confessing to some sort of crime against nature.

Nearly twelve years younger than she was. Ouch.

The coffee was ready, and she poured them each a cup. She was searching for something to say, but nothing was coming to mind immediately, and that was just making her that much more nervous, especially since visions of her sex dream kept popping up in her mind whenever she looked at him.

Luckily, he filled the conversational void. "You left the party a little abruptly. I hope it wasn't something I said or did."

Cat tucked an errant strand of hair that was blonde, much less due to nature nowadays than to Clairol, and didn't come to join him at the breakfast bar, preferring to put some distance between them and lean against the counter across the kitchen from him, gripping her mug like a weapon. He was just a little too much to take this early in the morning, especially after that dream. He was wearing a pair of black jeans that hugged him even more lovingly than the blue pair last night, with a gray T-shirt that had to be at least three sizes too small. It outlined every ripple in every muscle he owned, and it appeared that he owned a lot more of them than Clint ever had, or she ever would.

Chapter 4

When she realized she was staring, she grew mortified and blushed, which was even worse. Cat cleared her throat. "No, of course not. I just needed to get home."

Good going, brainiac. That was a blatant lie that any idiot who's known you for five *seconds could see through, and this man's known you for all of his life. You don't even have a cat to get home to!*

To her complete and utter horror, he rose and crossed to stand in front of her. "Weren't you feeling well?" There was genuine concern in his voice.

Lie. Tell him your stomach was upset. You had a headache. Athlete's foot. The heartbreak *of psoriasis—but he'd be too young to get that reference, wouldn't he? Wasn't that the heart of the problem, here?*

But lying didn't come easily to Cat. "No, I wasn't sick."

Finn stood stock still in front of her, not touching her, but very close. Uncomfortably so, but he'd trapped her neatly in the corner of her own kitchen, using her own discomfort against her. He didn't even need to use a hand on either side of her. He was so broad, he blocked her exit in either direction without having to put a hand on either side of the counter to do so. Unless he allowed her to, she wasn't going anywhere.

She was still staring at the ground, and he didn't like that at all. The last thing he wanted was to intimidate her in the least. He was big, but he liked to think of himself as a teddy bear, and he hoped other people—in particular, women—did too. A big, protective, if strict—in some cases—teddy bear. He'd grown up surrounded by women. His mom's large family had consisted mostly of sisters, and he'd had no grandfathers to speak of that he remembered, so the majority of his influences had all been females.

He loved women, no ifs, ands or buts about it. There was never any question in his mind about his sexual orientation, from as far back as he could remember. As he'd grown up— and up—and had filled out into a pretty bulky, muscular guy, all of that testosterone and sexual drive and basic male instincts had needed to go somewhere. He had been lucky enough, during those formative years, to have gotten close to Catherine's husband, Clint, to whom he credited the fact that he'd been able to navigate around a lot of the pitfalls of youth that his other friends hadn't.

Clint had treated him as a man from the beginning, even though he'd only been about fifteen when they'd started hanging out together that summer in his garage. They'd talked about everything, but one of their frequent topics, since it was always and forever on Finn's adolescent mind, was women. He'd adopted nearly all of his attitudes about women—well, those that his mother hadn't already instilled in him—from Clint. A man never ever hits a woman in anger or with his fist and only uses his strength to protect his loved ones. Also, that there would be one woman he would find whom he would need to love and protect and guide above all others, and she was the one he would want to be his wife.

And Finn had known, even from that early an age, that the woman for him was Catherine, and beyond some casual dating, he'd really not bothered to look much for anyone else.

She'd appeared infrequently in the garage, but always with some sort of baked treat and coffee for her husband, whom she always greeted warmly with a genuine kiss and true love in her eyes, and milk for him. She, too, treated him as an equal and never spoke down to him or changed the caliber of her language. Once, when she could see that he was confused by her choice of words, she'd gone into the house and come back with a dictionary that she'd said he could keep, and she'd helped him look up the word he'd been uncertain of the meaning of.

She was the most beautiful woman he'd ever seen at that age, and she still was, now, today, twenty years later. Nothing had changed as far as he was concerned. He'd stayed away as much as he could, knowing she was with the man she loved, and had ended up caught in California longer than he'd intended, due to business. But he was home now. He'd come home deliberately, although he'd always intended to eventually, to claim her.

And she looked like she'd seen a ghost. She was both pale and bright red at the same time, looking about seventeen in those disreputable pink sweats and that T-shirt that made him want to catch her and show her that he could be at least as good for her as Clint was. Maybe better, in a different way.

He knew she was freaking about the age difference, and he knew his mom probably would, although he really couldn't see why. He didn't care one bit, and he'd deal with the both of them in good time.

Catherine first, of course, in all things. That was the first tenet that Clint had taught him about serious relationships with women. And he had talked to him about just plain old sex, but he didn't dwell on it, saying any idiot could get laid anytime they wanted, that that kind of thing was entirely unimportant in life. Love was what was important, whom you loved and how you loved them.

'Your woman comes first, above your job, above the rest of your family, above yourself and your comfort. Always. You have to always do what's best for her, even if it's not what's best for you.'

"You left because of me, didn't you? I was making you uncomfortable."

Damn him. Wasn't the younger generation supposed to be self-involved creeps? Where was one of them when you needed them? Cat refused to look up or say anything. Maybe if she just concentrated hard enough, squinched her eyes hard enough, he'd go away. It had never worked on Clint, but maybe younger men didn't have such good defenses built up against things like that.

Finn reached out and lifted her chin forcibly but gently, although her eyes were still clenched closed.

Suddenly, she opened them. "Damn, you're still here."

He chuckled. "Sorry to disappoint you. You're going to be hell on my ego, I can tell."

Cat sighed, looking everywhere but at him. "You have to go away, Finn. Now. Please. Just… go away and we'll forget this all happened."

She didn't think there was any room between them, but he took a small step toward her. She could feel the heat of him, the already somewhat familiar scent of him. Her body remembered him from that blasted dream and began to respond automatically, to her disappointment, and she found it was something she could not control.

"Nothing's really happened yet, Catherine," he whispered huskily, cocking his head to one side, as if he was going to kiss her, but not quite getting to it yet.

"Please, Finn." She didn't want to sound like she was begging him, but that was how it came out anyway. She wanted to put her hands up and push him away, but she didn't want to touch him, so one ended up on the counter on either side of her, and he immediately covered them with his own, trapping them there but not hurting them in the least.

His mouth was dangerously close to her ear. "But we probably do need to deal with the fact that you just told me you had to get back to the house when you really didn't. And the fact that it was running through your head to tell me a fib about you having a headache, or cramps or something like that, just to throw me off the scent of you, off the fact that you want me, but you don't want to admit it yet."

How in hell had he known that? Was he reading her mind? Were they teaching that in schools nowadays?

Her startled look, the first time she'd met his eyes since he'd trapped her there, gave him his answer, and he smiled down at her, almost triumphantly but not quite. "I'm glad you didn't say it, though, because that would have been an outright lie, and it would have been that much worse for you."

"What would have been—" she barely got out before she found herself several inches off the ground, held securely against him by his left arm around her waist as he arched his back just a bit, and his free right hand came down on her largely unprotected bottom. She'd had the sweats she was wearing for years, and they'd grown so thin that they were quite threadbare in most spots, apparently especially the seat of them, since she yelped and yipped as loudly as if he was spanking her on the bare. Which didn't deserve thinking about in the least, despite the fact that it kept creeping into her mind at the most inopportune times, like right now.

It wasn't a long or arduous spanking, but it made its point and, worse than that, it was damned embarrassing for her, especially since he'd accomplished it so blasted easily, to say nothing of the fact that his rock hard arousal was pressed unrepentantly into her soft tummy the entire time. In fact, she would have sworn it had grown throughout the process. She had naturally tried to arch away from his swats, which meant that she ended up pressing herself obscenely up against him, even when his palm wasn't on her bottom. The spanking was quick, but it was very effective. He had her butt sizzling in just a few swats. She was afraid to wonder who he'd been taking lessons from, or worse than that, who he'd been practicing on!

But the worst part of it was less the physical pain of the spanking than the fact that it wasn't Clint who was administering it. If she'd really wanted just to be spanked by any old person, she could have found someone on the Internet to do it for her. They weren't that far from Boston, and she was certain that if she looked hard enough, she could have found someone to accommodate that particular taste.

But it had never been just the spanking that had turned her on. It had always been that Clint was spanking her. That her husband loved her enough to take his time and spend his energy to correct her that way. That idea had never ever failed —despite the severity of whatever discipline he decided to deliver—to make her slippery, and she had absolutely no interest in finding out whether anyone else had the same effect on her. In fact, exactly the opposite was true. That was something sacrosanct between the two of them that she never expected to share with anyone else, which was why she hadn't sought it from anyone else, why she hadn't actively looked for another partner, knowing that, in a vanilla relationship, she would be compromising—subverting—a very deep part of herself.

Finally, he set her down and stepped slightly away from her.

Despite the fact that there was no triumph in his eyes, that he wasn't gloating or obnoxious, and that he hadn't even tried to touch her since he'd brought her feet very gently to the floor, Cat was seething mad. No one spanked her but Clint. No one. It just wasn't done, and this young pup had tread upon sacred ground. He wasn't her husband, he wasn't even her boyfriend, and he wasn't likely to become either of those things.

Finn could see that she was angry in the way her fists were clenching and unclenching at her sides, and out of respect much more so than fear of any physical reprisal, he took a small step back.

Cat, who had been staring at her feet trying to collect herself and marshal her anger, raised her head and her hand at the same time, cracking her palm across his face and watching his head snap to one side with complete and utter satisfaction that was unlike any other she'd ever experienced. She wished she was a man for the first time in her life, so she could beat him to a bloody pulp.

"Don't you ever touch me again." She walked to the front door, opened it, and stood next to it. "Get out." Each word was enunciated perfectly, leaving no room for interpretation.

Finn cleared his throat and ran his hand through his hair, standing there in her kitchen for a moment, uncharacteristically indecisive, then he walked out the door. Cat slammed it behind him and didn't look out the window to see whether or not he'd looked back to see if she'd looked out at him.

He'd gone straight to his car, but there was a small smile on his face that he was glad she wouldn't see.

For her part, Cat had dissolved into tears, which she was very happy she hadn't done in front of him, and ran into her bedroom, throwing herself onto the bed and crying until her eyes were swollen shut and she fell into a deep, but disturbed sleep, where Finn, yet again, awaited, with his eager hands and fingers, and this time, mouth.

She awoke in a cold sweat in the middle of a Finn induced orgasm. The doorbell rang, twice this time, and she gathered that was what had awakened her. She walked to the door slowly, hoping that she wasn't going to have to fend off Finn.

But it wasn't him, and she wasn't quite sure what to do with the slight, let down feelings she had. What it was, instead, was a florist with a huge bouquet of at least two or three dozen long stemmed lavender roses and baby's breath, in a gorgeous arrangement in a big vase.

She tipped the deliveryman and took the flowers in to put them on display in the middle of her dining room table, wondering who in the world could have sent them. The card said "Catherine," and that should have been her first clue. The note simply said, "I'm sorry. Finn."

She had half a mind to throw them out, but they were just too beautiful. How had he known that lavender roses were her favorite? She couldn't resist leaning over to smell a particularly pretty bloom.

But the roses weren't enough to assuage her guilt about what had happened between them, despite the fact that, intellectually, she knew she bore no fault whatsoever. She began to spiral into a bit of a depression, despite the fact that another bouquet that was just as elaborate—with another variation of an apology—arrived the next day, and the next, until she was beginning to run out of places to put them.

And her friends were beginning to call repeatedly, probably because she hadn't been able to find the gumption to pick up the phone when they'd called the first time, either. Jane was threatening to come over, and that was all she needed. How, exactly, was she going to explain to Finn's mother that her son was sending her huge bouquets of flowers? That would not go over well.

Instead, he appeared on her doorstep one morning, when she threw the door open, figuring it was the florist. And it kind of was, because he was carrying his latest bouquet, but it was wildflowers this time; she recognized them as the ones that grew near his mother's house, as well as a casserole dish.

"Mom thought that you might not be feeling well so she sent over your favorite chicken casserole. Feed a cold, feed a fever. That's my mom." He smiled. "Are you sick?" he asked, not waiting for her to invite him in, but opening the inside screen door and gently forcing his way in by dint of his sheer size.

Cat frowned; she disliked being bullied. "I thought I told you not to come back here?" she said discourteously.

"No, you said I was never to touch you again, and to get out, but you never said I couldn't come back. Besides, I'd ignore it anyway." He made himself right to home, putting the casserole in the fridge. "I have a very good aural memory."

Cat just stared at him, crossing her arms over her chest defensively.

"A-u-r-" he spelled.

She glared at him grumpily. "I'm familiar with the word."

He nodded. "I should have known. Your intelligence is one of the things I've always been attracted to about you."

She decided she was going to let that pass. Suddenly, she was hungry. She shouldn't have been surprised, considering she hadn't eaten much in several days. "Which chicken casserole? The one with the stuffing and the mozzarella or the potatoes, carrots and onions?"

"The latter, I think. Do you want some for breakfast?" She was in what he assumed passed for pajamas, although it could be hard to tell with someone who didn't have to work. Sweats and t-shirts were the order of the day.

"You have to stop sending flowers. It's beginning to look like a funeral home in here."

Finn came to stand in front of her and realized that she looked thinner than she had, almost alarmingly so, and decided right there that she needed to eat something. He turned back to the fridge and put some of the casserole into the microwave for her without waiting for her answer. He'd feed it to her bite for bite if he had to.

"Am I forgiven?" he asked, leaning against the counter and crossing his ankles.

Cat swallowed hard. He really wasn't. It wasn't likely that she'd ever forgive him for what he'd done, frankly, and he might as well know that. "No. I can't forgive you for spanking me. Clint was and is the only man who spanks me."

He levered himself away from the counter and came to stand in front of her. "Oh, I wasn't asking for forgiveness for spanking you. I don't want forgiveness for that. It was the right thing to do. You need to be spanked. I want forgiveness for my, uh, bon… uh, erection. That was uncalled for." Finn smiled in a rakish, entirely charming and disarming manner that she hated because it melted her heart and was making it damned near impossible for her to continue to be as angry at him as she wanted to be. Not asking forgiveness for spanking her, but rather for his obvious sexual interest in her, what in the hell? "I couldn't help it, you see. You've been doing that to me since," he stopped abruptly when he realized he should be calling as little attention to their age difference as possible at this point, and changed his wording, "well, forever. And to finally have you in my arms. Clint was right. There's no feeling like it."

"Clint was right?" she parroted back at him.

"Yeah. You were the center of his universe, which is the way things ought to be in a marriage. He talked to me about you and your relationship a lot."

Cat swallowed hard. Surely, he hadn't talked to him about everything.

"He was the perfect man for me to be around when I really needed a strong male influence in my life. He helped me understand some things I was confused about—about women." He shrugged. "You know, guy stuff."

She nodded.

"He was a really special man. I can see why you're still mourning him." Before she knew it, he had her in a bear hug, and that was the perfect description for it. He dwarfed her, yet she didn't feel belittled or overwhelmed by his size. Instead, she felt protected and surrounded in a wonderful, loving way as he hugged her with just the right non-threatening, non-bone crushing pressure, then he let her go, pronouncing, "But that can't go on forever."

Realizing that he'd just completely ignored her edict that he never touch her again, Cat moved to the microwave to rescue her breakfast, saying ruefully, "Oh, it can't?"

"No, it's time for you to rejoin the living, and I'm just the man to help you do that."

Her raised eyebrow and smirk did nothing for his ego.

They sat across from each other at the breakfast bar again, while Cat picked at her meal, and Finn began to realize just how much of a watchful eye she really needed. She'd only taken about three bites before she put her spoon down and stopped eating.

He picked it right back up and started feeding her as he spoke, and she, startled, opened her mouth more out of surprise than anything else. "I know you think your life is over, and I understand that feeling. But there are still tons of things you need to do. Have you ever walked the Freedom Trail in Boston? Or spent Christmas in Quebec? Or spent some time in New York City? Or Vegas? Or seen the Grand Canyon or driven up the Pacific Coast Highway?"

She hadn't done any of those things, besides the short jaunts one took when one was on a field trip in school, which she discounted completely because all she remembered was trying to sneak cigarettes and beer the entire time they were supposed to be seeing Boston on their senior trip.

Finn got up and went over to her freezer and opened it, taking out the ever present pint of Ben and Jerry's. This time it was Strawberry Cheesecake, and he came to waggle it under her nose. "I happen to know that the Ben and Jerry's factory in Waterbury, Vermont gives tours and free samples. I'm surprised you haven't already made your pilgrimage."

She couldn't help it. She smiled. She didn't want to, but she smiled. But she also stopped eating, and there was still food on her plate.

It was Finn's turn to raise an eyebrow as he held up a spoonful of food and her mouth remained stubbornly closed. "I want you to finish this serving, Catherine. I didn't give you very much and you look like you haven't had a good meal in days. You've lost weight just since the last time I was here."

He was right, damn him, but how did he know that?

"Because I notice you."

Had she asked that question out loud? Her mouth was still closed.

"You have a choice," he said carefully. "You can either sit

there and eat the rest of what's on your plate, or you can sit there with a sore bottom and eat the rest of what's on your plate." Finn met her eyes calmly. "Your choice."

So much for not being able to be mad at him. She stood, nearly knocking down the snack bar chair in the process. "You cannot spank me."

He stood, much more slowly and deliberately, saying, "I'm sorry, honey, but that ship sailed five or so days ago."

Chapter 5

C at put her hands on the counter in front of her, leaning in toward him, not the least intimidated, which he loved. "No, it did not. You just spanked me. I didn't give you permission to do so."

Finn assumed the same position, leaning toward her, and said, "You hadn't given Clint permission the first time he spanked you, either. And you slapped him across the face for it, too. So I consider myself in very good company."

Her jaw nearly hit the marble countertop between them, and just as quickly, her eyes filled with tears and she turned away from him, hiding her face with her hands. "Go away. Please, just go away."

"No way in hell," Finn growled low under his breath, reaching her in two long strides and taking her in his arms, folding her right into them until she was all but lost against the sheer bulk of him.

Dear God, it felt too good to be in his arms. She didn't want it to feel so good. It was wrong to like it so much when it wasn't Clint's arms around her, which only made her cry that much harder.

She was breaking his heart. It was pulling into several disjointed, disabled bits right there in front of her, and she didn't even know it, nor did she much care, apparently. He could only hold her tighter but not too much so, just enough to let her know he was there and she was safe.

He wanted to take her into her bedroom and lay her down on the bed, to soothe her in the best way he knew how, with his body—his lips and tongue and cock. But perhaps that was just the fact that his libido was incessantly piqued around her. All he had to do was let a fleeting thought of her float through his mind and he was instantly and painfully erect. It was embarrassing, because it never happened to him with anyone else, and when he slept with other women, he was always thinking of her. He'd even made the rookie mistake—once and only once, of course, never, ever again—of accidentally groaning her name aloud, when the girl he was with was named Linda. Needless to say, he'd never seen *her* again.

And he hadn't seen many women anyway. That wasn't his style. Oh, he wasn't a monk, especially when he was younger, but as he grew older, he'd poured himself into his work more so than anything else. That alone, the monetary success he'd enjoyed in his line of work, had made him a target of the opposite sex, to say nothing of his size and good looks. But when he'd matured, and on the rare occasions that he surrendered to his body, he always made sure the woman knew the score in no uncertain terms. His heart had long since been spoken for, and there was nothing here for them on that account.

But now he was home and she was in his lap and his arms. He could touch her and had already spanked her, once, although it had been a somewhat dissatisfactory event, as far as he was concerned. He wanted the whole package. He wanted to be her husband and everything that came with that. When he was an adolescent and Clint had spoken to him of his love for his wife and their special kind of relationship, he'd found himself both turned on and touched in a way he'd never expected to be. Nothing he'd ever heard about or read had ever hit him in quite that same manner, and he knew it was right for him.

And, as he matured, he came to recognize that it was more than that, that it was Catherine herself who was right for him, whether or not he ever got a chance with her in this lifetime. He'd made up his mind, before he'd entered college, that he was going to do whatever it took to make enough money so he could come home one day and be around her, even if he had to include Clint in that equation. It would be enough just to be able to see her occasionally.

He'd heard of Clint's illness through his mother and had wanted to come home, but frankly, he was at a delicate spot in his business dealings, and he wasn't sure he could get away. Besides, they were both very private people and he knew that neither Cat nor Clint would have wanted anyone else hanging around them, and if they did, it wouldn't have been him.

When Clint had passed, he'd sent Cat a small arrangement —deliberately not of lavender roses—expressing his sympathies, but he hadn't been able to get away for the funeral, and in a way, he was somewhat glad of that. Finn wasn't at all sure he'd be able to trust himself to give her the time she needed to come to grips with the death, so he forced himself to stay away almost longer than he had intended.

But he was back now, and he intended to claim her in every way that was physically, emotionally, spiritually, and psychologically possible, and Clint's ghost was not going to get in his way. In fact, he liked to think that Clint would be happy to turn the reins over to him, as he fully intended to love and honor—and guide her—as much and as capably as he had.

She sniffled and sobbed, and he leaned over and fed Kleenexes to her, which she accepted gratefully. When the heartrending sobs had subsided a bit, she raised her head a little from his chest, her hair plastered against the side of it by her tears, and said in a watery voice, "You're still here."

Tears were still rolling down her cheeks, and it was all he could do not to cry, himself, at the sight, but he had to be strong for her. Without loosening his hold on her one bit, Finn reached out and brushed a hunk of it out of her swollen eyes. "Yeah, ain't that just a bitch?"

There didn't seem to be anything she could do to move this mountain of a man if he wouldn't go on his own, and he was wonderfully warm and comforting, so she let herself just put her head back down on his chest and fall asleep.

It was very hard for Finn not to jump up and down at that small victory, but he tried to satisfy himself by merely kissing the top of her head. To his delight, she fell asleep almost immediately, and he cursed very colorfully when, not five minutes later, the phone rang.

He took it upon himself to answer it, knowing it was his mother by the caller ID.

"Hi, Mom."

"Oh, you're still there?"

"Yeah, I stayed and made sure she had something to eat."

"Good boy!"

Finn rolled his eyes, trying to come to grips with the fact that he would never be much more than eight in his mother's eyes.

"How is she?"

"Tired and depressed and she's lost weight, so that's why I made sure she ate some of the chicken you sent. She's sleeping now. I was just about to leave." Her arm snaked around his waist to hold him when he said that, as if she didn't want him to go, and his heart melted further.

"Man, I hope she isn't slipping back into a depression like she got into just after Clint died."

Finn's interest was piqued. "Oh yeah?" He tried to play it off casually, but he wanted to know more.

Luckily, it wasn't hard to get his mother to talk. "Yeah, we were really worried about her there for a while. She didn't much deal with his illness and the inevitability of his death, I don't think, while he was sick. Once he died, it all hit her really hard. She nearly faded away to nothing right in front of our eyes. We need to make sure she eats."

Well, he had been planning on just tucking her into bed and leaving, but that settled that. He was going to make sure she ate something more—pretty much anything but junk food —before he left, and he was going to make sure that she ate regularly from now on, whether she liked it or not.

"Definitely. Can't have that," he replied, hoping he sounded casual enough.

"Well, I'll see you when you get back. Don't forget we're going over to Meme's."

"I won't. Love you."

"Love you too. Drive carefully."

"I will." As much as he would have loved to have let her sleep on him all afternoon, and even more so all night, he had other commitments today, and he wanted to make sure she got something more to eat before he left. He had a feeling there might be a bit of an issue about that, knowing Cat. He wanted to introduce the idea as soon as possible, so that if he needed to discipline her, they could get it done and over with and get her fed before he needed to leave.

He began to wake her, slowly and carefully, knowing how much she hated to wake up, especially abruptly. All through those summers he'd spent with Clint, he'd carefully catalogued in his mind every tidbit he could about Catherine, and he remembered nearly everything—likes, dislikes, pet peeves, preferences and opinions. Finn decided that the best way to wake her was with a soft, undemanding kiss.

She responded nicely, too, opening her mouth to the gentlest of pressures and making him moan at her warm, sleepy compliance. His hand found her braless breast, slowly, giving her more than enough time to raise an objection, but she didn't, as the edge of his thumb found an already pert nipple and she sighed slightly into his mouth. Her hands sought his hair, which he kept a little longer than Clint had, but as soon as those small hands found his broad shoulders and she woke up to exactly who it was kissing her, she jumped away from him like a scalded cat, standing well away from him.

"Don't do that!" She rubbed the back of her hand over her lips, as if wiping his kiss away, but it was that her lips were tingling from the feel of him. Her whole body was humming, and he'd barely touched her. She was cold now, from the lack of his body heat, and furious that she'd noticed it. What was he doing to her, dammit?

And he just sat there, grinning like an idiot.

"Don't you have somewhere to be?" she asked rudely.

"Not quite." Finn rose and went to her fridge. "What would you like to have for lunch?"

"Lunch? I just had breakfast. Don't you remember? You were here for it. You're too young for senility. That's my excuse."

He was disgustingly affable, to a point, still peering into her fridge and assessing the food situation. "Okay, then what would you like to have as a second helping of breakfast? Or a mid-morning snack? You have more casserole, hot dogs, some unidentifiable deli meat…"

Cat crossed her arms over her chest. "I'm not hungry, thank you. You can leave now."

He'd already graduated to rifling through her cupboards. "Spicy chicken Ramen, Oodles of Noodles, Spaghetti O's," he held the can up and looked back at her, "Spaghetti O's? Really? I wouldn't have guessed." Then he started listing things again, "Peanut butter, Fluff, raspberry jelly."

"You're too young to be deaf, Finn, but I just said I'm not hungry."

"PB and J it is," he pronounced, looking in her breadbox but finding it empty and turning back to her with a curious look.

"It's in the freezer."

"It's in the freezer," he repeated, finding it while mumbling, "of course, it is, Finn. She has a perfectly good breadbox, but she keeps the bread in the freezer, of course, you idiot. Doesn't everyone?" Setting the ingredients in front of him, he said conversationally, as he constructed a sandwich, "You should really put a note in there saying something like, 'See Freezer', so people don't get confused."

"People don't, since I'm the only one living here," she growled.

He put the sandwich on the plate, added chips from a bag on top of the fridge, and offered it to her, then snatched the plate back from her. Not that she was reaching for it anyway. "Do you like your chips with your sandwich, or in your sandwich?"

"It's not my sandwich, so make it whatever way you like." Cat shrugged her shoulders.

Finn placed it on the snack bar and said quietly, "I've said it before, and I'll say it again, Catherine, as many times as I need to. It's your choice whether you eat with a sore bottom or not."

He was glad glares couldn't hurt him, or he'd be stone cold

dead, but then he actually watched her stubborn set in, and her jaw clench.

"I am not hungry, so I am not eating that sandwich. Make of that what you will."

What he made was her butt very sore, and her eat the sandwich, and he barely moved a muscle doing so, because she hadn't noticed—being years out of practice and all—that he'd already moved his foot onto the rung of the bar stool he'd pulled out in front of him when he put the sandwich down, in anticipation of her defiant answer. Clint had told him she could be stubborn sometimes, that occasionally she got something in her craw and just decided she needed to prove her point to him that she was an independent woman, when there was never any doubt in his mind—ever—that she was a very independent woman. He'd never considered that the fact he spanked her diminished her in any way, least of all, her independence.

But as he'd said, she sometimes couldn't get her head around something he really wanted her to do, almost always something that truly was for her own good—go see a doctor for a test, or take a particularly disgusting medicine, or some such thing, and she would flat out refuse to do it. It went against her usual affable nature, but then, everybody had their quirks. It was up to him—the man who loved her—to make sure his woman didn't cling to quirks that could get her into trouble, and if she did, then she needed to be corrected, in no uncertain terms.

Finn had her over his raised knee, baggy knit pants around her ankles where she definitely didn't want to encounter them, followed alarmingly by her pretty and delicate purple flowered panties.

"Are you out of your mind?" she yelled and wiggled and tried to hit him, but he'd already maneuvered the chair well out into the kitchen, and himself well out of the way, so there was nothing for her to hit, and nothing for her to latch onto to assist herself in any way, either.

"Bastard!" she yelled.

"Ah ah ah," he chided, giving her a very hard swat, and she embarrassed herself completely by fairly bellowing because of it. "Watch your language, Catherine. You'll find I'm a good deal less lenient about that kind of thing than Clint was. You always had much more of a potty mouth than I would have let you get away with," he leaned down a little toward her, but not enough to do her any good, damn him, and corrected, "than I *will* let you get away with."

Each swat made her wish, more than the one before, that she had just eaten the blasted sandwich. Why couldn't she just have eaten the friggin' sandwich? She always ended up regretting it when she got stubborn like this. Always. It never ended well for her—or her backside—and yet she always let herself get her back up about something stupid, not that she'd ever admit that any of her various causes were stupid. On the contrary, she would defend them to the death.

But she ate the blasted sandwich. Standing up. While glaring daggers at him. As he stood there, smiling beatifically back at her and making her several more sandwiches for later.

And it didn't help that he was so darned pleasant about it all. He did a good job blistering her bottom, at least as well as Clint would have in the same situation, she hated to admit. Then he'd helped her up very carefully, pulled up her pants and panties, although she'd brushed his hands away, whereas she wouldn't have with Clint since he would never have let her get away with that, but then, he was her husband. Finn poured her a glass of milk and was disgustingly solicitous of her the entire time. He was awful, and she hated him.

Well, she wanted to hate him, anyway. That counted for something, as far as she was concerned.

"Finish the milk, too," he prodded gently, poking the cup toward her.

If she didn't stop frowning, her face was going to set into that expression permanently. She had half a mind to take the big mouthful of it she had in her mouth right now and squirt it back out at him, but then she caught him looking at her as if he knew exactly what she was thinking, with his eyebrow all raised expectantly. She remembered how that right hand of his, that was right now cradling a can of soda, had felt against her bare rear and thought better of it as she swallowed it all down. It sucked to realize there were consequences to her actions, again. It sucked big time.

"Thank you. You'll feel better for having something in your stomach. I've left you with Mom's stuff and two more sandwiches. When I come back tomorrow, I expect it all to be eaten."

Who did he think he was, laying down the rules for her, telling her what to do? He was just the neighbor's kid—

She was hauled up against him in an instant, her feet dangling well above the floor, her body plastered against his. He was only using one arm to hold her at her waist and seemed entirely unfazed by the added weight, as if she weighed no more than a housefly. Cat could feel the entire length of him against her—both of them—and knew he was fully capable and probably had been from the moment he'd stepped in the door. Come to think of it, she knew he had been. It had been hard to miss when he'd come into the house, and then he'd put her on his lap where it had been extremely blatant, and now, here he was again, in all his turgid glory.

His mouth sought hers, and to her shame, she didn't even try to avoid it but rather joined his kiss eagerly, so much so that he leaned back a little and looked at her, as if verifying that it was still her, then bent to her again, deciding he didn't want to consider his luck too closely. Finn's free hand claimed her everywhere he wanted; he gave it free rein. He clenched what he knew had to be a tender bottom cheek that fit his hand just perfectly at its rounded peak, then let it travel up the curve of her back, under her shirt, reveling in the soft skin of her back, then diving into that sweet smelling hair of hers to hold her head still for his plundering tongue.

Finally, he had to set her aside or he'd take her right then and there, on the floor of the kitchen, and that wasn't where he wanted to make love to her the first time. So he set her down and stepped away from her, panting and unable to stop feasting his eyes on her. "Dinner tomorrow in Bangor. Think of an out of the way restaurant where none of your friends are likely to go. I'll be here at six." He gave her that look, along with his card, on the back of which he'd scrawled his cell phone number. "I'm not kidding about wanting you to eat that food," he restated in a tone that made her butt tingle.

Then, with one last long, luxurious kiss that had him biting at her lips near the end and had him barely able to pry himself away from her, he was gone.

The phone rang while she was just standing there in the middle of her kitchen like some dazed schoolgirl who'd just had her first French kiss. She'd forgotten what a Grand Central Station this place used to be.

Of course, it was Jane. "Is my son still there?"

"No." Cat cleared her throat, hoping Jane wouldn't notice the hoarseness of her voice. "He left."

"Good. We're going over to see Meme."

"Oh, that'll be good. Listen, thank you for the chicken dish. It's my favorite."

"I know. Did you have some?"

"Yes. Finn can be," she searched for the right words, "very persuasive."

Jane chuckled. "Yeah, he can be, when he wants something."

Cat bit her lip and shut the hell up on that one.

"He's worried about you, and so am I. He said he thought you'd lost some weight and were depressed again. Are you?"

She cleared her throat again. "No, just sad."

"You're clearing your throat."

Dammit. That was a clear tell that she was hiding something, but she never realized it until after she'd done it a couple of times. Bloody hell.

"Okay, really sad."

"Oh, Cat, I'm really sorry, but you've just gotta snap out of it. Get out and do something. You're spending entirely too much time at that house. Are you taking your antidepressants?"

"Yes, Mom."

"Good. Well, then we need to get you out some. Lemme see whose turn it is to have the girls over."

"Okay."

"And lemme ask you something, since you've spent some time with Finn."

Uh-oh.

"Do you think my son is gay, but is just scared to tell me? I mean, he hasn't had a girlfriend in so long, I don't remember the last one's name. And he's never even brought a girl home for me to meet."

Dear God. The absurdity of the question, and who she was asking it of, made her want to snort in Jane's ear, but she managed not to. "I don't think so, Jane. Maybe he's just not comfortable with being sexual around you at all—hetero or not. And you've told me yourself that he's been flat out building his business. He doesn't have time for a girlfriend. You know how those nerdy computer types are."

"Yeah, well, I don't want him to be alone, you know, especially since I've found my Ted." Jane had the "happy couple syndrome" that made her want everyone with whom she was close to have the happiness that she and Ted had found.

"I understand. But I don't think you have anything to worry about with Finn. He was out in California to make his way, make his mark in the business world. Probably, since he's back here, he'll settle down, find a girl and have a family."

That was exactly what Jane, who was dying to become a grandmother, wanted to hear. "Oh, from your lips to God's ears!"

They made plans to have lunch in a few days, then hung up.

Chapter 6

Cat decided that the two of them, for what it was worth, were right. She needed to get out of the house. So she took a ride to the top of Cadillac Mountain and walked around up there a bit, heartily enjoying the fact that the mountain kept trying to blow her back off. Then she walked along the Acadia National Park Loop Road a bit, although most of it was closed off since it was still early yet and not quite tourist season, but it was still gorgeous.

Then she headed home, her mind full of thoughts about Clint and Finn and what she was going to do about the two of them. Or rather, the one of them who was still alive and trying to date and/or spank her.

———

"Yeeee-owww!" Okay, mental note—her next boyfriend was definitely going to be older than she was. And decrepit. Emphasis on the decrepit. Like not able to raise whichever hand he favored to spank her. That sounded like a very good idea to Cat right now, especially since the man who was currently indulging in that activity was disgustingly young and even more disgustingly muscular and fit.

It had been a while since she'd been really spanked. Clint had been actively sick for quite some time, and that part of their relationship had had to take a back seat for the last four or five years they had together. They had both mourned the loss, but that was the way it had to be. She'd forgotten how absolutely horrid it was, but someone was in the process of helping her remember it. Someone who had told her to eat all of what he'd left for her in the fridge—the two pb and j sandwiches and what had turned out to be enough chicken casserole to feed the Third Army.

She'd managed to eat some of the chicken and one of the sandwiches and was learning very quickly that that was far from acceptable, as far as he was concerned. Imagine that—a dominant man who wanted her to do precisely as he'd said. How noble. She'd forgotten, happily, it seemed, how they could be such sticklers some times, and it was even worse if they thought what they wanted was for her own damned good.

What was she doing here? Her panties were around her ankles yet again and she was over his lap on her own blasted sofa, which she was happy hadn't seen much action from herself and Clint since they'd bought it after he'd become sick. At least there were no comparisons going on in her mind from old memories flooding her brain. That was something to be very thankful for. She'd cancelled this date, for crying out loud. Or rather, she'd tried to.

Cat had spent an awful, sleepless night, dreaming of the man whose hand was rapidly searing her cheeks but delivering an even more blistering and humiliating lecture. She was mortified to realize, but late this morning, she'd called him, trying to break the date. They shouldn't date. It was just not right. He was too young, she was too old, they were too different, they were just... too. Too attracted to each other, too explosive together, too likely not to make it out of the house to go on the actual date for one reason or another, but she wasn't about to go there with him over the phone or she'd never be able to talk him out of it. She had a feeling it was a lost cause anyway, but she had to at least give it a try. She'd made up her mind. They couldn't possibly date, and she'd decided to inform him of that fact in a serene, rational, and mature manner.

He'd been very calm but had reassured her, in no uncertain terms, that they were going be going out not only that evening, but many others, and he was going to arrive on her doorstep exactly when he said he was, to take her out to dinner in whatever condition she happened to be in at that time. If she was nude, then she was going nude. If she was in pjs and bunny slippers, then she was going in pjs and bunny slippers.

Cat had uttered a longsuffering sigh that had come alarmingly early in this relationship, and he had chuckled low in his throat back at her in a most unsettling manner, igniting every nerve ending she possessed. Tired of fighting with him already, the brat in her resurfaced for a moment. "Oh, all right," she'd said ungraciously, turning off the phone without even saying goodbye and immediately delving into her closet for something to wear. Since she really hadn't been planning to go out with him, she hadn't given her wardrobe much thought.

She had a lacy pink concoction that she'd bought several years ago on a whim that would probably fit the bill, although it might be a bit too sexy. She should really be wearing something toward the frumpy side, to discourage him. But the pink dress looked fabulous on her if she did say so herself. And she did, but rarely, like most women.

She'd been wandering the mall—an unnatural pursuit for her, but she was bored—and saw it in a shop window. It was on sale, which made it even more appealing. Cat loved a bargain, even though she had no one to wear it for and nowhere to wear it to. It had hung in the back of her closet, untouched since then, too pretty to wear to the places she usually went.

She hauled it out now and put it on, glad to see it still fit like the proverbial glove. In fact, it was even a slight bit big if she let herself admit it. She frowned. Damn him, he was right. She did need to eat something. She was losing weight, not that she'd ever admit that to him under any circumstance.

Light makeup, the small, drop diamond earrings Clint had given her for one of their anniversaries, and a pair of flats that were just the right complementary color completed her ensemble, along with a very light spray of perfume just as she'd heard the doorbell ring.

She checked her watch—six exactly. She liked a man who was on time or even a little early. Cat detested lateness in anyone, since she was compulsively early herself. Her mother had always said it was because she was making up for being three weeks late to her own birth. But then, she thought as she'd made her way to the door, he probably already knew that. It was kind of disconcerting that he knew so much about her—even little peccadilloes and preferences—when she knew so little about him. If they were actually going to continue this "relationship," she'd try to rectify that tonight. But they weren't, so she wouldn't. She was still determined to convince him that it wasn't a good idea at all that they date.

She opened the door and then just stood there like an idiot for the longest time, staring at him with her mouth open, drool puddling at her feet. The man was friggin' gorgeous, there was no way around it. How the hell had he latched onto her, anyway? She knew he didn't have a Mommy complex; Jane had raised him better than that, and besides, he spanked much too hard for that. Pretty soon, there wasn't going to be enough hair dye in the world to cover her gray, and she already couldn't finish ninety percent of the sentences she started. He was going to be bored with her in a half an hour; maybe that would be her out.

But damn, he was a fine looking man!

He was wearing a sport jacket that strained just slightly across those football star broad shoulders, as did the white shirt beneath. He was wearing dark blue jeans that clung lovingly to every muscle of those thick legs like she wanted to, and she was surprised to see the tips of cowboy boots on his feet. He'd gotten a haircut, and it was noticeably shorter than it had been, which she definitely preferred. His face showed no stubble, no soul patch, no artfully shaved beard, nothing but his square jaw and sensuous lips, until she worked her way up to those chocolate brown eyes, which were gently laughing at her. "Can I come in, or do you need me to strip down out here before you decide?"

Completely mortified and raspberry red that he'd caught her so blatantly salivating over him, Cat opened the door and stepped back so he could walk by her, giving him plenty of room to do so. Still, he barely scraped by, deliberately dragging himself up against every bit of her so that she got a feel of every inch of what she'd just taken an eyeful of, and he watched every second of her reaction to him with a lazy, self-satisfied smile on his face that made her want to punch him.

She couldn't suppress it. It was too big for her—lots of it, probably, she thought with a twisted smile—and she let herself go with it, arching against him, letting her head fall back and enjoying the feel of his body against hers.

Finn wanted to lay her down right there, in the foyer, in front of the full glass door where God and anyone who bothered to drive or walk by could see them, but he didn't. He contented himself with teasing both her and himself with that little body rub, then turned and continued straight into the kitchen.

Cat closed the door, expecting to see him in the living room, but he'd gone all the way into the kitchen for some strange reason and was peering intently into her refrigerator.

All of a sudden, she remembered. She was supposed to have eaten all that food he'd left for her—both of those sandwiches and a boatload of casserole. Or, at the very least, destroyed the evidence to seem like she had. Fuck.

"What did you just say?" He'd already started back to her, with a look on his face that said he wasn't happy that she had disobeyed him, and shortly, she wasn't going to be, either.

Oh, crap, had she said that out loud? She was going to have to be a lot more careful about her language from now on, dammit. But no, they weren't going to be doing this again after tonight. "Nothing." Cat hoped that came out sounding as innocent as she wanted it to.

"I should hope not, considering you've already got a spanking coming for not eating what I told you to eat, Catherine." Finn had come to stand right in front of her.

Darn, he was big when he stood over her like that. It made her want to take a step back, but she refused to do it. This was her house, and she wouldn't be intimidated in it, certainly not by him. "I ate what I wanted of it. I had a sandwich and some of the casserole. There was too much of it for me to eat in twenty four hours."

Finn had seen that flash of fear in her eyes, and it almost made his resolve crumble. The last thing he wanted to inspire in her—ever, ever, ever—was fear. He knew he was a big lug of a guy. He couldn't help that, and she was a very small, delicate woman. Even more so, he thought, when she was wearing such a fairytale dress that suited her perfectly, but it just served to accentuate her fragility. He felt that if he reached out to touch her, she'd splinter into a thousand tiny pieces.

He took a step forward, remembering that she hadn't backed away from that luscious body greeting they'd had in the doorway. "You are so beautiful," he breathed against her ear. "That dress was made for you." She smelled the way every woman should, and he buried his nose right behind her ear, touching her nowhere else, and breathed deeply of her scent —a very light, floral perfume, used sparingly, a soft shampoo, but mostly just Catherine, a mixture that he found entirely intoxicating.

When he straightened, she was blushing again, or was that still? One end or the other of her seemed to be permanently red around him, not that he was complaining on either count. He wanted her so badly, he could barely think, but he knew he had to maintain his priorities. She would come to count on him to guide her, and the heart of that was consistency. If he said he was going to do something, then he needed to do it. This was something in which he would not—could not—fail.

Finn took her hand and brought her to the living room couch, standing her directly in front of him. He reached up under the skirt of her dress and gently, carefully, relieved her of her panties, which were little more than scraps of lace that somehow perfectly matched the color of the dress, as if they'd come as a matching set. They didn't sell them to women that way, did they? He wondered fleetingly.

Cat had tried to protest, weakly and ineffectively. Finn knew it was a necessary gesture on her part and simply brushed her seeking hands away carefully but inexorably. He wasn't sure if she'd been actually trying to stop the spanking, or if she was just trying to keep him from baring her bottom again. Probably a little of both. It must not be easy for her to be that intimate with him so early on in their relationship—

bare bottomed and over his lap, as she was seconds after he'd brought her undies to her ankles, well away from any easy retrieval by her.

This would be the first time he'd really be able to take his time with her. The first time he'd really see her and be able to touch her. He discounted her other spankings as more quick and expeditious. This one would be more deliberate and ritualistic, although not quite as much as he would like. Finn understood, from Clint, how important that element of discipline was to Catherine, that the rituals were a big part of what made her feel safe and secure, beyond himself and his presence, and when their relationship was more cemented, he would certainly implement those.

Right now, though, he indulged himself as much as he could, slowly raising the gossamer skirt of that cotton candy dress while she reached back and tried to stop him. He caught her wrist easily, trapping it in his free hand at the small of her back almost as an afterthought. Cat had tried to kick her legs, but the panties at her ankles kept her legs trapped nicely together, just as he'd intended.

Her bottom was a thing of perfection. He'd never, ever think of her as an old woman; he'd never considered she was much older than him, frankly. Finn had never thought much about age as pertaining to a woman, anyway. Unlike the majority of his sex, he was attracted to personalities first; looks were a distant second. Luckily, with Catherine, he got both. Despite the fact that she was too skinny—hence the reason for her being in this position, he thought with a deep frown—her bottom was as generous and well-rounded as he could have asked for, which meant it would only become more so as he helped her out of her depression. He was truly a lucky man.

Right now, though, he needed to take care of his woman, even if she might not see it quite that way—the taking care or his woman, just yet.

Finn believed in spanking hard while he was chiding a woman, so he started right in, peppering his lecture with solid, heart—and bottom—felt swats. "When I tell you to do something, Catherine Angelique Taylor, I expect you to do it. I don't want excuses. You're entirely too thin, and you need to put on some weight and eat healthier. If I have to buy you groceries and make you breakfast, lunch, and dinner, and come over here and feed them all to you forkful by forkful, don't you think I won't."

She definitely wouldn't put that past him for a minute. He was at least as stubborn as his mother was, maybe more so, and that was not a compliment. At this point, she wouldn't put much of anything past this man, dammit. Cat was trying desperately to wiggle her way off his lap, but he was a big man and had long legs, and it was a depressingly long way off them, to say nothing of the fact that his free hand held her easily in place, so all her wiggling got her was more swats for too much of it.

"Stop that right now, Catherine. You're going to get a thorough spanking, and I'm going to make sure you get every swat that's coming to you, so you'll think twice the next time you decide to ignore something I've told you to do."

Finn landed a long series of crisp, firm swats to her rounded cheeks, alternating spots and sides, and that was the impetus for Cat's loud "Yeow!"

"You've been much too long without someone keeping his eye on you and his hand on your bottom, but that has come to an end right now. Your end. I can promise you that your lovely little backside is going to be getting the attention it deserves from now on, Catherine."

Oh, dear, now he was slapping the backs of her thighs! She hated that almost worse than the spanking itself. It was bad enough to be spanked on her bottom, but the backs of her thighs were what she thought of as more innocent territory, less capable of handling the swats that a bottom might normally be expected to endure.

She wasn't going to give him the satisfaction of crying. She wasn't. But when he'd ripened the entirety of her backside to a cherry red, then began again and reminded her in a horrible, chiding tone that couldn't possibly have come from a man who was more than a decade younger than she was, that she was going to be reminded of how naughty she'd been when she had to sit on her bottom at the restaurant, she burst into tears.

That was what Finn was waiting for. He issued several sharper, well placed spanks, mostly right where her bottom joined her thighs, so she definitely would be reminded while sitting demurely across from him in the restaurant. Then he pulled her up and into his arms, not letting her arrange herself yet, but holding her tightly against his chest and rocking just a bit, patting her back and letting her cry it out.

He had a packet of Kleenex in the inside pocket of his jacket, for just such occasions, and gave her one immediately. Then he went back to patting and rocking until she leaned away from him just a bit, even though she was still sobbing slightly. "I have to fix my makeup."

Cat would have stood up, but Finn caught her hand and looked into her eyes. "Just a second. You have something to say to me before you go."

She blanched, her eyes widening then filling with tears again that overflowed down her cheeks in true rivers. She knew what he meant. It was what Clint required of her, that she express remorse at having been disobedient.

Finn wasn't at all sure he really should be pressing her at this point, but it felt right, and he usually went with his gut in most situations and was proven right nine times out of ten. He didn't push or press, just waited for her to work things out in her mind and held her hand while she did it. She didn't have to be elaborate or thank him—that might come later, he hadn't decided—but he did want her to say she was sorry, and he knew that she was aware that was what he was asking.

She hung her head for a moment, and he was seconds away from relenting. He thought his heart would never stop aching from the sad, dejected picture she made. But then she raised her head and looked him straight in the eye, saying softly and very quickly, "I'm sorry for not eating more."

Finn nodded, and Cat reached down and removed her panties more efficiently than he would have imagined that tangled mess could have been dealt with and fairly ran to the relative safety of the bathroom. He turned to sit in the corner of the too small for him, fussily flowered couch, looking out at the river below, silently thanking Clint for talking to him the way he had when he was younger and giving him the opportunity to love Catherine now.

When she reappeared, her face was flushed and her eyes were swollen, but she had never looked lovelier to him. She made her way to the door, but he stopped short at what he presumed was the coat closet, making her pause at the door. "Are you ready?"

Finn gave her a look that was hauntingly familiar. "I am, but you're not. It's barely the end of spring in Maine, and you need something, at least a light wrap, or you're going to get cold."

Cat was frowning more at the fact that he was right than the fact that he was dictating to her again. That wasn't good. She stomped back to him, and he opened the door. She took out a light dress coat, and he helped her into it, then gave her his arm and escorted her to his car, which she couldn't help but admire. Her parents weren't poor, but they hadn't had the kind of money that got her the sports cars of her dreams.

Apparently, though, Finn had that kind of money. His car was a newer Porsche 911. Not quite the latest hybrid she'd read about on the web but a gorgeous, catch me if you can, red machine, nonetheless. She'd have to hide her Nissan in shame, rather than park it next to his.

The ride over to Bangor was about thirty minutes, and Cat had to admit she had been a little worried about what the heck they were going to talk about, but it seemed that Finn had no such concerns. He kept up a steady flow of conversation the entire time, sometimes talking to other drivers, which she found amusing since she did it herself a lot—although she used much worse language—and other times asking her questions about what she liked and disliked, what her favorite movies and television programs were, the usual first date questions.

They found they liked a lot of the same movies, agreeing that Godfather I and II were the best movies ever made, and that III was some sort of atrocious aberration and should be forgotten altogether. They were both involved in Lost and Heroes, but he watched Survivor and American Idol and she'd never seen either of them, whereas she watched Project Runway and Top Chef religiously and he'd barely heard of them.

They settled on a classic rock station out of Bangor to listen to on the way—I95—and Cat found herself automatically playing a game that she and Clint used to play where they challenged each other to name the song and the artist that played before the other person did. They'd been pretty evenly matched, considering they were born less than a year apart and grew up listening to the same songs.

Chapter 7

W hen the next song came on and began with four snaps of someone's fingers, she had it before the second snap, blurting out entirely without thinking, *Queen, Killer Queen*, and earning herself two points.

Finn gave her a questioning glance. "Huh, what?"

Embarrassed, she explained the game, and to her surprise, he was keen to try it and was more than a worthy adversary.

Annoyed that she was losing, Cat said, "How come you know all these songs? They're well before your time!"

"Consider the source; you know how many albums my mom has. Guess what I grew up listening to."

"Oh. That's an unfair advantage. You're younger and you have a better memory." As she recalled, Jane did have a prodigious album collection, since she'd gone to work as soon— sooner, really, than was technically legally allowed by law—as she could, both to help support her family and to earn some spending money for herself.

Princess Cat, on the other hand, hadn't started working until she absolutely had to. Mommy and Daddy had supplied her every want and need. It was nice to be a princess, she thought, until she shifted in her seat and felt the soreness of her bottom, remembering that some of those who were princesses in their early life ended up paying for it—in one way or another—when they were older.

She'd chosen a small, out of the way restaurant that she and Clint had never been to but that she'd read good things about online. It wasn't actually in Bangor; it was north of there, in Orono. It was well known for its steaks but offered a variety of classic homemade foods in a beautifully restored mansion that lent an intimate atmosphere to the dining experience. At least chowhound.com said so, anyway, so she was going to trust Hungreeinme's opinion of the place and give him or her a piece of her mind later if it stunk.

It did turn out to be a gorgeous house, and Cat loved old houses that had been refurbished to their former beauty. She would have preferred if it had remained a house, rather than being transformed into a business—or worse, apartments— but at least it hadn't been torn down. They were given a seat by the bow window in the room that had probably been the front parlor at one point, and their waitress was wonderfully attentive, not that they were paying attention to much of anyone but each other.

He'd pulled out her chair to seat her, whispering in her ear as he did so that he could request a pillow for her if she liked, enjoying the way she flushed so beautifully at his wicked comment.

Finn offered to get them a bottle of wine, but wine wasn't much to Cat's taste so she wrinkled her nose but encouraged him to get one if he wanted. When they'd ordered—prime rib for him and a filet for her, after she'd tried to get away with just a bowl of seafood chowder that got her a look that had her bottom tingling uncomfortably in the straight backed chair —he moved the place setting out of his way and put his elbows on the table to lean toward her, gazing directly into her eyes. She did the same, mirroring him, if only on a whim.

Then he asked something that stopped her in her tracks, because it seemed he was reading her mind, yet again. "So, is this the time when you try again to convince me that we can't possibly date and try to kiss me off as if this is going to be our only dinner together?"

Cat choked and reached for her water, although it wasn't much help.

"That's what I thought."

"But…" she wanted to explain. She hated arguments and confrontations, but she'd had all her reasons lined up, not the least of which was her friendship with his mother. And he'd gone and taken all the wind out of her sails, the bastard.

He leaned back, palms on his thighs, awaiting the challenge with relish. "C'mon. Out with it. Let's get it over with. I don't want it hanging over us forever." Finn's eyes narrowed, and she felt the weight of all of that considerable focus on her. "Because I'm not going to let anything stand in the way of us, Catherine. Nothing and no one."

She leaned on her arms again and played her trump card. Might as well get it right on out there. "Not even your mother?"

There was absolutely no hesitation in his response whatsoever, and Finn was extremely close to his mother. "No. Not even my mother, although I have to tell you that I have no worries in that area, either." He reached across the table and took her small, cold hand in his, slipping it between both of his to warm it. "Catherine, I'm not fifteen, and you're not some predatory school teacher or something like that. I'm thirty four—"

"Almost," she corrected.

He smiled. "Almost. And you make me very happy. What more has my mother ever wanted? Why should she care who I marry? She just wants me to get married to someone."

"Thanks," Cat deadpanned. "That makes me feel so much better."

He grinned. "You know what I mean."

"She wants you to have children. She wants grandbabies out of your marriage, and I'm really too old and, frankly, not very inclined to have children at this stage in my life, Finn. Have you thought of that?"

Their waitress arrived with their salads and left as unobtrusively as possible. The food went untouched. "Yes, I have. I don't want children, either. And if we decided to later on, we could adopt."

Cat shook her head. "You're my best friend's son. You're too young for me. Your mother would kill me. When Title IX was passed, she wanted to play on the boys' football team, and they would have let her if it weren't for your nana."

His face went completely blank; Title IX became a law well before he was born.

Cat sighed. "I rest my case, but needless to say, if we ever got involved, your mom would kill me dead." Jeez, did that sound as adolescent as she thought it did? "Besides that fact, she's my oldest and dearest friend. She's like the sister I never had. I don't want to lose that friendship." By the end of that sentence, her eyes were filled with tears, and she was looking anywhere but at Finn.

Finn's low voice melted relentlessly into her ears. "Think of your bottom, Catherine. We're already involved, and there's no way I'm going to walk away from you now. I've waited too long for you. I'll handle my mother and make sure that nothing affects your relationship with her."

She raised her head and looked into his eyes with tears trailing down her cheeks. "But how can you do that? You don't know how she'll react to this."

"I think I have a pretty good idea. But first things first—I want you to agree to date me for a little while before I talk to Mom about it." He motioned toward her salad plate and took up his own fork.

Cat sniffed and bit her lip, tapping her fork against the side of the plate. "And what if I say no?" she asked tentatively.

Finn calmly finished his mouthful of salad, leaned closer to her, and said quietly, "The same thing that happens when you don't eat your sandwiches and casserole, Catherine Angelique." He watched her shift uncomfortably in her seat.

'I don't have much of a choice in the matter, then, do I?"

He cleared his throat. "No, you don't." Finn didn't much like where this conversation was going. "Look, Catherine, if I felt you honestly objected to me as a man, to intimacies with me, then I wouldn't be pushing so hard. You would have screamed bloody murder from the moment I introduced the idea of spanking you. But you've already been extremely inti-mate with me, in a manner that is peripherally sexual. You're not the type of woman to put up with that if it's really not something that you want." He put his utensils down and asked her a question point blank that had been niggling at the back of his mind for some time. "Have you dated anyone else since Clint died?"

She was playing with her food, moving it around the plate rather than eating it, and he would deal with that in a moment. "No," she whispered, staring at the swirls her fork was making in the raspberry vinaigrette.

"So, no one else has…"

Cat's eyes shot to his and she blushed that beautiful, vibrant pink of hers. "No, of course not!"

"But you've let me do it. Several times. With barely a squawk of protestation. Doesn't that tell you something?"

She wasn't sure if it did or it didn't. She wasn't sure of anything anymore, except that she was very unhappy at the thought of losing a friend she'd had almost forever, in favor of a man she was just barely starting to get to know, no matter how gorgeous and how potentially compatible in an unusual area he might be.

Finn reached across the table and put his hand on her arm. "I want you to stop thinking about this right now and let me handle it for you. I'll take care of it. I want you to just let go of it, and date me for a while. We'll skirt around here for a very short time, I promise, long enough for you to decide whether this is going anywhere." It killed him to say that, because he knew that she was the love of his life, but she didn't have the same feelings for him yet, which was understandable because she hadn't spent her whole life waiting for him.

But he knew she would, and he knew that, regardless, he had to give her the choice, or it wouldn't be right. He couldn't force himself on her; she had to accept him, especially considering the deeper elements of what would be their relationship.

He kept the rest of the meal toward a much lighter tone, although he did maintain a very watchful eye over her eating habits, encouraging her to eat rather than play with her food. He went so far as to tell her that he wanted her to clean her plate when it arrived with a petite filet, garlic smashed potatoes with a touch of sour cream, and fresh green beans.

Cat glared up at him and swore there was no way she could put away that huge amount of food, but he kept her laughing and talking throughout a dinner that lasted twice as long as she was used to, and by the time the waitress came around to collect their plates, hers was completely clean.

"Very good," he praised.

She gave him the evil eye. "Don't get used to it."

Finn chuckled. "It's your bottom." He took up the dessert menu. "Shall we indulge ourselves?"

They did—in a wonderful lemon tart that was the perfect complement to their meals. They were barely able to waddle out to his car, where Cat joked that he was going to need to use a shoehorn to get her in.

The ride home was quieter than the ride to dinner had been, but it was a pleasant, comfortable silence. He held her hand on his thigh the entire way in a familiarity she'd never shared with any other man but Clint. Finn didn't wait for her to ask him in but took the keys from her as soon as she'd dug them out of her purse and let the both of them in.

He helped her out of her coat, hanging it neatly in the closet, then before she could escape, he turned her and pulled her against him in one smooth move, his lips claiming hers as he bent her backward just enough that she had no choice but to cling to him for balance.

Cat's head was spinning, and she couldn't even blame it on alcohol. She could lose herself in him so easily, and that was exactly what he was encouraging her to do, of course.

Finn wasn't going to give her the chance to think about much of anything. He intended to press his advantage wherever he could, and he wanted to make love to her tonight. He needed to feel that closeness with her and wanted her to experience it with him. He wanted to lay claim to her, in the most primitive manner that he possibly could.

She was in his arms before he could think twice about it, and within a few strides, they were in her bedroom. Cat hadn't made a peep, not that he'd given her much of a chance, though. His mouth had been plundering hers the entire time.

The way he set her down onto that cream, rose, and celery green comforter said a lot to her. She felt as if she was a piece of bone china, the way he made certain that she was comfortable and he didn't accidentally crush or lean on any part of her. He followed her eagerly down, cradling her face with his big hands.

"Do you know how beautiful you are?" he asked huskily, his eyes roaming over her reverently.

She knew he was lying, of course. She knew it. She'd forced herself to contemplate her figure very carefully in the mirror this morning after her shower, in anticipation of the possibility of this very moment, and it wasn't a pleasant sight. She was no spring chicken, and certain portions of her anatomy no longer resided quite where they were supposed to. It was no wonder ninety nine point nine percent of Hollywood had themselves nipped and tucked. Gravity was, indeed, a bitch.

But you'd never know there was anything amiss by Finn's behavior. His hands were everywhere, but he wasn't a groping teenager. His touch was light and sure, over her clothing at first, as if he was gentling her for later things, letting her settle to his hand before he went any further. Finn's mouth rarely left hers, and when it did, she could barely bring her mind around to think about anything, although she knew she should. She shouldn't have let him do this, shouldn't be in this room with him, shouldn't have gone on the date with him. The list was becoming endless, but there was no end in sight. He already had her half out of her mind with wanting him; all his hands and mouth had done was tease her, bring her ever nearer an edge she hadn't seen in quite some time. Her body was more than ready for him—much more so than her mind, and it was her body that was in firm control right now, welcoming him with wide open arms and open legs, regardless of how insecure she felt about him seeing her nude.

But he was wonderful. She still had all of the scented candles and oil lamps that she and Clint had collected placed artfully around the room, and he left her just for a second to light some of them, as well as bump the heat in the room up a bit, cautioning her with a frown to stay put. The soft, ambient light was perfect to ease her concerns—much better than any harsh, overhead light. Not, of course, that Finn cared in the least, but he knew she did, especially when she began to realize what his next step was.

She did keep trying to brush his hands away when he returned to lie beside her on the bed, and at one point, he didn't say anything, but rather reached beneath her to grasp her still sore bottom cheek and look deeply into her eyes. The hands that had been not quite deliberately interfering in what he was doing fell away immediately to lie almost submissively by her sides, but not quite. Finn nearly smiled. He didn't think he'd ever be able to think of Cat as submissive, and that was fine with him, as long as she did as she was told, one way or another.

Finn took every stitch of clothing off her, first, while he remained fully clothed, except for his jacket and shoes. She assumed a virginal pose, covering the usual strategic areas, but not at all for the same reasons. When she looked at herself, she automatically catalogued every imperfection that he might possibly see, especially in comparison to some nubile twenty year old whom he really should have been with. Cat covered her breasts because they weren't as firm as she would have liked them to have been. They weren't around her knees, but they weren't quite as perky as they had been when she was twenty. And her other arm was less aiming to cover her privates than it was the slight swell of her belly, that, to her, was absolutely enormous, despite her recent weight loss.

Of course, he wasn't going to allow her to prevent him from enjoying any part of her. She was his, and he intended to impress that on her this evening, as many times as he physically could, and continue to do so until she could see it for herself.

On the other hand, he also didn't want to bully her. He wanted her to come to the realization by herself, but with whatever help was needed from him to guide her in the right direction. It seemed, however, that he had a distinct ally in her body. She writhed every time he kissed her and kissed him back with all of the fervor he could ask for. He could see, peeping out from behind her upper arm, her nipple was peaked, and her sweet breath was coming in soft pants.

She wanted him, whether she liked it or not, and he intended to capitalize on that, reaching out to brush the tip of his finger over the distended tip of her breast. He heard her shocked, indrawn breath, and she tried to arch away from him, but he wouldn't allow it. Instead, he caught that impudent tip and held it, not tightly, not painfully, but just held it, so that she couldn't move away from him.

It made her drop her arms away from her body and concentrate on retrieving her nipple and her own indignation, which was his intention. "Finn, stop! You can't look at me, really. I'm not pretty anymore, I'm old!"

Finn carefully but deliberately maneuvered her wrists until they were pinned by her head in a classically submissive position that he didn't necessarily favor, but that got the job done, saying, "I feel several rules coming on about not putting your looks down, not trying to stop me from touching you, and calling yourself old. I'm sure I'll come up with a few more if—"

Out of self-defense, Cat raised her head and kissed him before he came up with any more edicts, but then she ruined it by saying, "I can't help it. I only speak the truth."

She found herself flipped over onto her tummy in seconds, his hand claiming her rear as it already had earlier this evening. "I can still see the imprint of my hand on your wonderful butt, but I'd be glad to warm it up for you, if you feel the need..."

It was interesting that he was leaving the choice up to her. Sort of. But not really, because in the next instant, that redwood palm connected with her already tenderized rear because she was taking too long to answer him.

"All right, all right, already." Her feet beat a bratty tattoo on the bed. "I won't do that anymore."

"And what won't you do, sweetheart?" he asked, his lips kissing the area he'd just scourged.

Cat twisted her head to look up at him and said in all seriousness, "You can't ask a forty five year old woman to remember that kind of thing, honey. I won't do whatever it was that you just told me not to do. I'll remember the details later, in the middle of the night, when I don't need them."

He dissolved into laughter but swatted her twice, hard, as he reminded her what she was agreeing to, then he flipped her back over and claimed a nipple with his mouth, suckling greedily. And then he stopped, for no reason Cat could discern. He leaned away from her, his hand lying possessively on her stomach, unable to keep his hands from playing with her breasts.

Cat was moaning and wondering what she'd done that had caused him to stop suckling, and she gave him a quizzical look.

"I just realized we haven't talked about what we like and don't like, and I don't want to do something you don't like."

She rolled toward him, hoping things shifted into some resemblance of a reasonable looking order. "I think you can safely assume that what you were about to do is definitely acceptable. And my list of don'ts is probably a lot shorter than you might think."

"Really?"

She wasn't at all sure she liked how amazed he was at that thought. "Yeah. Did you think I was going to be that high maintenance—'don't touch me here, oh, I couldn't possibly do that'?"

Her simpering tone had him laughing, but it was almost uncomfortably close to some of the younger women he'd dated. "I really didn't know what to expect, frankly, but I want to know."

They lay together, on their sides, facing each other.

"Well?" Finn was nothing if not impatient.

"Jeez, gimme a minute. I've never had to come up with this list."

He was amazed. "Never? Didn't you have to, you know…" He really didn't want to bring her dead husband into the bed with them, but it seemed somehow unavoidable at this juncture. "Tell Clint?"

There was that luscious shade of pink again that made him want to nibble her all over. "I was a virgin with Clint. I didn't know what I liked or disliked, beyond spanking, really."

He was intrigued. "How did you know you liked that?"

Cat snorted. "I was an advanced reader, and my parents let me read pretty much anything. My mom had a huge stock of those historical romance novels—bodice busters. You know the ones, with Fabio on the cover, but before he came along. That was back when quite a few of them were A. not much better than soft core porn, and B. had spanking scenes in them. So I scarfed every one of them that had a spanking scene out of her bookshelf and got her to buy me more. Even some of the mainstream, like Harlequins, had spanking scenes before they became more 'enlightened' in the eighties."

He wasn't sure he wanted to know the answer to this question, but he asked it anyway. "How old were you then?"

She shrugged. "Too young. Way too young. Young enough that I really didn't know what I was reading about, at first. Eventually, I began to read only by author because I knew which ones wrote books that contained the scenes I would be interested in. One of them turned out to be a man, which I thought was interesting. I haunted the used bookstores in Ellsworth and Bangor religiously, looking for more fodder for my overactive imagination."

Filing away all of that information about her, Finn kissed the back of her hand. "So, what would you say are your likes and dislikes?"

Chapter 8

She became an even more brilliant pink if it were possible. "Uh, I like most things. I like oral, both ways, but not sixty-nine. It just feels really… forced to me, in either direction. I feel like I can't concentrate on what I'm doing or on what's being done to me. There's just too much going on."

Finn smiled and nodded. "Any other positions you like or don't like?"

Cat tilted her head while she was thinking. "No, not really. I hate to sound all stodgy and vanilla, but I really do like missionary the best."

"Good," Finn pronounced. "So do I."

Thinking again, Cat said, "I don't think I have to say anything that involves those who can't consent?" She looked up at him.

"Of course. That goes without saying."

"Face. Do *not* lick my face." She actually shuddered at the thought, and he knew he was going to need to remember that. "I don't know what it is, but that really bothers me. I'll lick yours, if you like, but just don't do mine."

His eyebrow rose. "Anything else in particular you don't like done to your face, or on your face?"

"No. I just don't like tongue on my face. Cum is fine."

Well, that answered that question.

"What about you?"

Finn was deciding that he liked this position, so he divested himself of his clothes, finally, which, as he'd hoped, helped her feel free to explore him, and he adored her touch. Her fingertips teased incessantly because her touch was so light, but he was learning to endure it. He could see it was going to be a lifetime of low-level arousal around her. "Oh, I think men's lists are pretty nonexistent, beyond the nonconsensual. If they're honorable in the least." He was busily trailing his own fingertips up and down the very sensitive inside of her right arm lazily, as if he hadn't a care in the world.

"I guess I could say that I don't much like having my toes sucked. I had a girlfriend once that was really into feet, and it got her off to spend a lot of time down there, but that's just not my thing." He took a distended nipple into his mouth and suckled hard for a moment, then released it and soothed it with the tip of his tongue. "Now that's my thing." Finn looked up at her. "Your moans, your hard nipple in my mouth, on my tongue, feeling the way you're panting as I'm pleasuring you. Your reactions to what I'm doing get me harder than anything but your touch, and all I want is more of both."

He pushed her over, onto her back, and she was powerless to stop him, not that she felt the need. He wasn't threatening her in any way; he was simply being a very primal male. He rubbed his face all over her, as if he was marking her with his scent, nibbling on the more interesting areas he found until he encountered the triangle of hair between her legs.

Cat knew that she was out of vogue. She wasn't supposed to have any hair there at all, and if she did, it was supposed to be shaved into something cute or interesting or funny, or waxed to within an inch of its life. The mere thought made her cringe. Her pubic hair was fair, like the rest of her body hair, and barely noticeable. More so the more she aged, and the older she got, the less likely she was to futz with it.

Clint had never cared about it, and he was the one who was confronted with it the most. She was the least likely of the two of them to do anything about it.

"Sorry about the thicket," she felt compelled to say, certain that he'd probably never seen such a jungle, considering that the clean shaven look had been in style for quite some time.

"Stop that." He frowned up at her. "I'll let you know if you have something to feel sorry about."

Cat didn't like the sound of that idea at all and frowned back down at him, but she couldn't hold it when his mouth descended upon her and he reached beneath her to use her hips to pull her toward him. Her legs fell away, naturally, and his shoulders held them well up and back, granting him unrestricted access to every intimate inch of her.

He was ready. He was more than ready. He'd been ready for her since before he was really capable of dealing with a woman of her caliber. Yet here she was now, lying before him, open and yielding, allowing him to pleasure her and take her for his own, trusting him with the honor of all of herself. It was almost overwhelming.

He could smell the rich scent of her, feel her heat, see the moistness he had created within her. He had done that to her, made her ripen and swell to his touch. His mouth teased at first, raining butterfly kisses over that entire exposed, vulnerable area, making her moan and arch and plead wordlessly for his favor.

"Shh-shh-shh, my love. In a minute. These things cannot be rushed," he whispered against the inside of her thigh before biting it gently, then he wandered back down to the secrets hidden inside those distended lips. He was of a mind to press his fingers inside her, but he decided against it. He wanted to open her with his cock, knowing it had been a good long while since she had been made love to, and wanting to feel that gloved tightness around the steely length that was clamoring for his own end. But not before hers.

Finn ruthlessly clamped down on his own desire and pressed a loving kiss directly on top of that burgeoning bud, licking it gently back and forth with only the very tip of his tongue. He could hear her moans at being treated that way, knowing it was nowhere near enough to give her what she wanted. She was demanding, his love, keening and nearly crying in her desire for fulfillment. It was music to his ears.

"Please, Finn...please..." she cried.

"Oh, darlin', you don't have to beg; it's coming, it's coming," he crooned, settling better into his spot and addressing her more seriously, fingers of one hand holding her wide open for his greedy delectation while the other reached under to remind her that she'd been spanked not too long ago, squeezing what was probably a still aching bottom cheek.

It was more than Cat could bear. Much, much more. She'd held off for as long as she could, not wanting to sully Clint's memory, not wanting to give in, not wanting to let go of him and taint what they'd had together, but Finn was relentlessly pushing her past all of those self-imposed barriers with his calmly dominant attitude and his warm, wet mouth.

When she finally contracted beneath those all too knowing lips and fingers, it was unlike anything she'd ever experienced before. It wasn't one big explosion and then a lot of little reverberations, it was one gigantic explosion that seemed to go on and on and on, never diminishing in intensity at all. It went on so long that Cat began to get scared, and the person she would normally turn to wasn't there.

Finn was very attuned to Catherine, but he hadn't been expecting this. There was no way he could have anticipated it. When he realized what was happening, all thoughts of his own pleasure dissolved in the face of trying to reassure her that she was okay.

She seemed to be trying to leave, which he wasn't about to allow, so he simply caught her and rolled with her, gathering her in the bedclothes and swaddling her against him. She was crying, and it was horrid. He'd thought it was bad when she cried when he spanked her. This was a million times worse, especially since he wasn't exactly sure how to help her. "What can I do, honey?" He held her tightly against him.

"T-tell m-me t-to s-stop," she shivered out.

"Stop?" he asked densely. "Stop what?"

"Com-ming!"

Instead of doing it immediately, Finn had to stop and think about that. In some ways, women had all the luck. What he wouldn't give to be able to engage in a nonstop orgasm. Who was he kidding? If that was possible, he'd never leave the house. Hell, the whole male population of the planet would never leave their house.

"Finn!"

"Stop, baby, stop. I want you to do as I say and stop coming right now, Catherine, or I'll flip you over and give you a spanking." He wasn't at all sure if the threat would help, but he figured it couldn't hurt, and he would certainly do it if she needed it.

She'd stopped shaking and spasming almost immediately. Finn was kind of proud of himself for the achievement. He'd never given a woman a continuous orgasm before. Hell, he'd never even heard of one before now.

"Are you okay?" he whispered against her ear.

She just nodded, still crying silently.

"I'm sorry," they both said at the same time, then laughed somewhat awkwardly.

"What do you have to be sorry about?" Finn asked. "It was your orgasm."

"Well, you gave it to me," Cat answered, laying her head on his chest where it was already wet with her tears.

"I guess there's really no harm, no foul, with an orgasm, but I'm sorry it scared you. I take it that's never happened before?"

She shook her head. "Never. Usually it—well, it's a big first contraction and then smaller, like aftershocks, and then it just kinda fades away on its own, but this one's intensity never abated. It just kept going and going."

"The Energizer Bunny of orgasms. I like that." He liked it better that he'd made her smile.

"You okay?" he asked for the umpteenth time.

"Yeah. Sorry for the interruption in what has otherwise been a wonderful evening." Cat reached up and kissed him on the lips a little tentatively, then with more passion.

It didn't take much to spark Finn's interest again, but he didn't want to be an insensitive pig. "Are you sure you're okay?"

In answer, she kissed him again, more deeply this time, then reached down between them and gently grasped him, ruining the effect by giggling at the way he moaned uncontrollably at her touch.

"I'm going to have to remember that the next time you're threatening to spank me! I have a secret weapon to use as a diversion!"

He rolled them both just slightly so she was on her back, inserting his legs deliberately but slowly between hers, giving her more than enough time to object if she needed or wanted to. "Oh, you might succeed in that at first, but remember, I'm younger, and I have a better memory, so you wouldn't get away with it for long."

Cat frowned. "Hey, that ain't right! That's another reason why we shouldn't be together. I need someone my own age who's more likely to forget my transgressions than remember to correct me for them."

He'd brought her legs up and back farther than she would have thought they'd go but hadn't entered her yet, although she could feel the head of him pressing insistently against her.

"Look at me, Catherine," he commanded, his tone far from the teasing one he'd just used.

She did as she was told.

He didn't say it, but he didn't want her thinking of Clint when he took her for the first time. Finn wanted her to watch him, to acknowledge and know in her heart that he was the one who was making love to her. He wasn't going to allow her to use him as a substitute for Clint.

Dear God, he was enormous! Or maybe it was just that it had been a while, but he was stretching her almost to the point of discomfort, despite the ample butter her body was generously providing.

Each soft keen, the way she gripped his shoulders and half mewled, made him want to plunge himself into her to the very hilt. But he refused to do so. He wanted this possession to take a long time. He didn't want to hurt her, and he wanted her to remember every second, every millisecond of it.

Finn hooked her legs over his elbows, forcing her back even farther, forcibly lifting her bottom off the bed and opening her even further to him as he let his body weight do its job. Their eyes never wavered from each other. He could see that she was just short of pain, just shy of it, riding that edge carefully, and when he finally stopped, he rocked in just that much harder, pumping with his hips, pressing and shifting side to side, fitting himself into her completely while she gasped and moaned and fought to accommodate him.

He couldn't help it. He threw back his head and roared, his body taking over as he began to delve in and out of her, hard thrust after even harder thrust. Until a humiliatingly short time later, he roared again, uncontrollably, and collapsed on top of her, completely spent and unable to move.

Finn had never, ever lost control of himself like that before. He had always kept himself under a tight leash, especially when he was in bed with a woman, mostly because of his size. Now, here he was with the woman he'd waited his lifetime for, and he'd let loose on her like some kind of savage. He'd practically raped her, and he'd screamed like a banshee. She would probably throw him out of the house and never see him again.

But instead, he realized that her hands were making lazy patterns on his back, sometimes massaging, which felt absolutely wonderful, and sometimes just trailing her fingertips over his muscles, which didn't feel too awfully bad, either. She didn't seem to be in the least mad at him.

He rolled off her and to the side, certain that he was also crushing the life out of her with his size. The majority of the women he'd slept with had complained if he didn't get off them pretty much immediately after finishing, so he'd gotten used to doing that.

Cat rolled toward him with a small smile on her face. "Good thing we bought all of the lots around us for miles or we'd have Sheriff Potter to explain ourselves to, I'm sure, and that old coot'd be having a good time with our story, too." She patted his arm. "It wasn't continuous, but it sounded pretty good?"

She was asking him if it was okay? He wasn't used to that,

either. Maybe he'd been dating some pretty awful women, or something. The girls he'd slept with always seemed to assume that they were great in bed—they didn't try very hard—because he always came. "Oh yeah!"

She laughed at his vehemence.

"Sorry about… the quickness."

Her snort was surprising. "Puh-leeze. If you're not going to worry about a little hysteria on my part…"

He wasn't going to tell her how long it had been for him because talking about premature ejaculation was uncomfortable at any time for any man, and it hadn't been quite as long for him as it had for her, but it had been a while. Finn was certain that he'd be more than fine in the future. Like probably about fifteen minutes from now.

The next morning, she awoke alone, but he'd left her a note and, of course, more rules.

My love,

Words fail me at the trust and faith you've shown in me in such a short time. Know that you are treasured beyond measure.

I have business in Boston and will be gone until Saturday night, when we'll go out. I've made plans for everything, so nothing for you to do but be your gorgeous self.

You are to eat three nutritious meals a day and keep track of your weight to tell me about when I get home.

I know you'll think it's too early for me to say this, but I love you.

Yours adoringly,

Finn

. . .

The purple roses arrived right on time, this time five-dozen of them. And then an edible fruit arrangement, a cookie basket, and the gift boxes and baskets just kept right on coming. One had old time candies from the seventies—Bottle Caps and Clark Bars and Laffy Taffy—things she would have sworn they'd stopped making years ago.

He called her at least once a day, usually two or three times, just to check up on her. It was kind of sweet of him to do that and nice to have someone doing it again. Not that she'd ever admit that to him, of course. He asked her what she'd eaten and what she weighed, and she'd earned herself another spanking on the first phone call the first night when she hadn't weighed herself that day. And claiming early senility hadn't gotten her out of it, either. There had to be some advantage to being old in this relationship, didn't there?

So this weekend was going to be a busy one for her. It was a girls' night weekend at her house, suddenly. She didn't know how she'd let that slip by her, but she did. And Saturday, they were apparently going out somewhere she knew nothing about and about which he was not being very forthcoming. He'd just told her to "wear something nice." It was probably a good thing he couldn't see her rolling her eyes at him.

Girls' night consisted of a floating pool of women, but usually a core of about five of them who had known each other for way too long. They all knew about most of the skeletons in everyone's family closets, going back generations. In some cases, their mothers had had girls' nights, although they'd called it bridge night or game night instead, and they'd drunk a lot less and sworn a lot less than their daughters and granddaughters.

Jane had shown up first, of course, but luckily after Cat had hidden all of Finn's excessive gifts in the back bedroom, where no one was likely to go, although she had used some of the excess in the snack trays. Why not? She certainly wasn't going to eat all of that food by herself by any means.

Everything seemed fine with Jane, although Cat had nearly dropped the bowl of chips she was bringing to the hutch that served as a buffet table in the open dining room when she mentioned that she thought that Finn was dating someone because he'd been gone all night. She seemed positively giddy at the thought, but Cat found herself wondering exactly how giddy Jane would really be if she confessed right here and now that she was the one Finn had been schtupping that night.

Rhonda Bates floated in next. She was a fey woman who never seemed to really know what was going on around her. Life seemed to pass her by, always had. And she wasn't even on drugs or anything, as far as anyone else could tell. If one was going to be that hazy, why not just take the drugs and enjoy it? She was just... not really all there, and her shambles of a life reflected it.

The three of them sat down at the table and started playing, knowing that the last member who would probably show up would be traditionally fifteen minutes late. At least. Girls' night usually started at seven, but Carol Potter couldn't be counted upon to make her entrance until seven fifteen, at the earliest, although seven thirty or seven forty-five weren't entirely out of the question. She was, after all, the daughter-in-law of the chief of police and had been a beauty queen in her younger, salad days, lest anyone be allowed to forget it. She carried herself as if she was always wearing that blasted crown—stiffly and uncomfortably, and with an eye to how the peons were reacting to her.

But she could be a dear friend when she wanted to be. While Clint was sick, she did all of the stupid errandy things that Cat was apt to forget—paid Central Maine Power and the gas and the cable and Harvey, the snow plow guy, and the paperboy. All out of her own pocket without ever hearing of letting Cat pay her back in any way.

"What'll we play till the queen arrives?" Jane asked, lighting a cigarette and taking a deep drag. Ted wouldn't let her smoke at home.

"Waft some of that over here, will you?" Cat said, taking a deep breath as Jane blew the smoke in her direction.

"He's gone now. You can smoke if you want to."

Jane knew about Cat and Clint's lifestyle. She didn't approve, but she knew about it.

Done with all of her futzing now that everyone had their drink of choice, the hors d'oeuvres were out and the games were within reach, Cat slid into a chair. "I don't want to. It's bad for my health. You know I get instant pneumonia when I smoke." She took another deep breath full of second hand smoke. "I just miss it sometimes."

"Poker?" Rhonda suggested.

They usually played either poker or Triopoly. Everyone arrived with their spare change either rolled or in unique bags or boxes, hoarded away from their children and husbands so that every six weeks or so, they could all get together and drink and smoke and laugh and exchange it with each other, 'cause that was what it boiled down to.

Carol made her entrance at about seven twenty-five and watched as her friends exchanged the money right in front of her that meant they had bet on when she would deign to arrive. "Bitches," was all she said, with absolutely no rancor as she sank into her seat.

Cat got her a scotch on the rocks and a bowl of Cheetos, the hard ones, not the soft ones, because she knew that was what Carol liked, and received a beatific smile for her efforts. "You spoil me."

"I do, but someone else got there first, and only the first

round is on me. You'll have to crawl to it yourself the next time."

They played poker for a while, and Cat won, which was somewhat embarrassing when she was the host of the party, but she had great luck at cards. And it was dumb, blind luck, because although she wasn't stupid, she had no great affinity for poker. She didn't keep track of the cards that were played —that was entirely too much work. She'd never really learned how to play the game properly or played online at all, but she got good hands, and that, apparently, counted for a lot.

It also helped that the people she was playing with got drunker than she did and didn't pay attention to the fact that she rarely bluffed, so if she stayed in a hand and bet large amounts, they really should have folded.

By the time they stopped playing and everyone had adjourned to various bedrooms in various states of inebriation, she'd won almost all of the money on the table. Not bad for a night's haul.

Chapter 9

Breakfast the next morning, by tradition, was at a little hole in the wall place that served breakfast only, but it was right on the water and its breakfasts were enormous. They also served Bloody Marys, which was Carol's only requirement. The waitresses all knew them, and they had a standing table and order whenever they arrived, off-season, of course.

As the rest of them tucked into buttermilk pancakes with real butter and real maple syrup—the only time they allowed themselves to indulge all month—the talk turned, as always, to town gossip. Someone mentioned that a woman they all knew was seeing a man who was a few years younger than she was, and she was instantly labeled a cougar.

Cat choked on her coffee at that, and everyone turned to look at her. "Got something to say about that, do you?" Rhonda prompted.

"First of all, I hate that word. Secondly, a few years older does not make her a cougar, and thirdly, age shouldn't mean a thing any longer, just as race doesn't, as long as all parties are above the age of consent." She'd said her piece, and she was going to back the hell away from the subject, but Cat was also surreptitiously watching Jane's reaction. Everyone's—including Jane's—heads were nodding in agreement, so she was going to take that as a good sign.

The man in question was still calling her all the time, except last night, which might have gotten the ladies suspicious. But there was a message waiting for her on her machine when she got home. He'd called her from the airport and just said that he loved and missed her and was looking forward to their date tonight.

Cat wasn't at all sure what she felt about him professing his love. She knew he didn't want her to feel pressured by it, but that was kind of hard to avoid. It was something she knew they both took seriously. He'd never married, and she was beginning to suspect that she was the reason. What if she and Clint had lived to a ripe old age together? Would Finn never have found a woman to settle down with because she was already taken? She didn't like to dwell on that idea because he was a really great guy—minus his right hand.

And she still wasn't at all sure about how she felt about the fact that she'd hopped into bed with him on the first date, either. She might be a bit old fashioned, but that just wasn't done when she was dating back in the Stone Age. Of course, she and Clint had been pretty much in courtship since they were in diapers, and he had been the only man she had been close to until Finn. She was a virgin on their wedding night, for crying out loud. And now here she was, at the ripe old age of almost forty-five, sleeping with Finn at the drop of a hat.

At least pregnancy wasn't a worry. She had already been told six ways to Sunday that she couldn't conceive, and she hadn't. It had never been a problem with Clint, since they didn't want children anyway, but that was another cause for concern with Finn. She had a hard time thinking that he wouldn't want children at some point down the line, and she already knew Jane wanted him to want lots of them, if she had her way.

When he picked her up that night, she had spent all day worrying about their situation, mulling it over in her head, worrying about it like a sore tooth, unable to leave it alone. To his credit, he picked up on it immediately after giving her a wonderful kiss hello, as if they'd been separated for months rather than days.

"What's the matter?" He eyed her critically, as if looking for cracks or lumps, then he began to run his hands down her, feeling for breaks like a paramedic.

She tried to wiggle away.

"What are you doing? Stand still."

Cat continued to squirm, until he administered several quick swats to her jean clad bottom.

"You know better than that. What did I just say?" He swore, sometimes it was like dealing with a five year old.

Finally, she stood stock still, mortified at the words that had just come out of his mouth. "You said to stand still." It was something that Clint wouldn't have hesitated in saying, but hearing those chiding, slightly paternal words coming out of the mouth of a man who was so much younger than she was, was humiliating and, at the same time, an alarmingly hot turn on. What a perv she was!

"Then what are you to do?" And where did he get that stern tone of voice that had her legs quivering and her insides turning to jelly.

A heavy, put upon sigh. "Stand still." He gave her a thorough going over, even squatting to check her legs and feet surely and carefully. "Jeez, what are you, a doctor?"

"No, but I was a volunteer EMT for a while." But he

wasn't going to let her distract him. He tipped her chin up and made her look at him. "What's up?"

"Nothing."

She found herself clamped against him in an instant, his hand swatting her bottom again steadily.

"You'll find quickly I hate that kind of an answer, Catherine. It was a real question, and I want a real answer, and the spanking doesn't stop until I get one."

Damn, who had taught this man to be dominant? Oh, right. Damn Clint for being so good at what he did. And damn Finn for learning so blasted well!

"I've been worrying."

His hand ceased its spanking immediately, and he was all concern and caring again. "About what, honey?"

Cat was much more worried about the condition of her bottom at this point. He was spanking her an awful lot. Jeez, he'd only been in the house less than five seconds, and he'd already spanked her. That was some 'honey I missed you'!

"About us, about this, about the whole thing. I'm just concerned. I know you said I shouldn't be, but I am. I can't help it. I'm a worrier. That's what I do."

Finn smiled slightly and hugged her tight. "Forget about it for the rest of the weekend. I'll deal with it as soon as I can, and it will be resolved, and we can go on with our lives. Okay? You'll see. It will be a non-issue."

Cat thought he was glossing over it, and she was sure he thought she was making a mountain out of a molehill. But they would see whether or not her relationship with his mother would survive this. Dear God, if they got serious and she ended up marrying Finn, Jane would be her mother-in-law. She shuddered. She couldn't bear the thought of that.

He frowned down at her. "Okay?"

"Yeah."

They stopped in Bangor at an Asian buffet and ate themselves into oblivion, then continued out into the back of beyond, to a tiny bar where a band he used to be in was playing. They were now a country-dance band. When he was with them, they'd been an eighties band.

They danced, both very badly, and she drank—he refrained entirely since he was driving—and the guys recognized him and called him up on stage to sing a few numbers for old times' sake. She was surprised to see him pick up an acoustic guitar and step up to the microphone. He sent a couple of power ballads out to her, and Cat had the satisfaction of seeing much younger women drooling over a man who only had eyes for her and who sang every word of every song while staring right to her.

When he finished Air Supply's *Every Woman in the World* and climbed down off that stage and into her arms, the crowd erupted in applause, and she could feel the daggers from the looks from the younger women sticking out of her back.

They left while they were still clapping. As the gravel crunched beneath his boots and her shoes, he leaned over and whispered in her ear, "Someone has a spanking coming for not weighing herself when she should have."

If her lower lip had protruded any farther, they would have been tripping over it. But he just chuckled at her expression and tucked her into the passenger's side of the car. Cat fumed. She'd been looking forward to getting home and making love to him, but now she wasn't so sure.

She didn't want to be spanked. She'd never really wanted to, and Clint had understood that. She thought Finn probably did, too, but it seemed that neither one of them would ever tire of teasing her about the fact that she did get spanked and that they were the ones who did it.

Cat hadn't much been paying attention to where they were going. She had a bit of a buzz on, not much but some, but he was perfectly sober and she didn't have to pay attention to how he drove. Besides, it was damned hard to get lost going to the Island. There was only one road there. But he made an unusual turn, and they ended up somewhere that she didn't expect to be—Hadley Point Road, where they could drive right out onto the beach. It wasn't open ocean, but it was certainly beautiful by the bay, and it smelled of the sea the way no other ocean but Maine ocean did.

But apparently, they weren't there to tourist. Finn had something else in mind all together. It was nearly dark, and it wasn't warm enough for anyone else to be out there but them. He felt relatively safe that they weren't going to be disturbed, so he got out of his side of the car and came around to hers, helping her out.

"What are we doing?" she asked, just slightly tipsily.

He took his coat off and spread it over the hood of his car, right next to where she was standing. If she hadn't been slightly hammered, she would have already discerned his intent, but that was working nicely in his favor or he was sure she would have been screaming her head off by now. "Didn't I just remind you before we left that you have a spanking coming?" he asked, almost casually.

"Yes, but—" That was as far as she got before he bent her inexorably over the jacket-covered hood of his car.

"Finn, no! What if someone comes down here!" she hissed, as if there was already someone potentially listening to them, although there were no houses anywhere near the area.

He'd already thought of that, of course. "I've angled the car so that we'll see anyone's headlights long before they arrive, love. And you know as well as I do, it's too early for the tourists to descend."

Son of a bitch! He was really going to do this! Clint had always threatened her with something like this, but he'd never actually done it. Finn was taking things to a new level—a new, uncomfortable level.

But when she tried to stand up to turn around and talk to him about it, she found his hand on her back, preventing her from doing so. "Finn, I'm scared!" Cat didn't realize that what she'd said would have such an immediate reaction from him, but she filed that away for future reference.

She was instantly gathered in his strong arms, coat and all, shielded against him, and away from any potentially prying eyes. "Honey, I would never put you in any danger at all, under any circumstance, for any reason. If I think it's safe, it's safe. I've waited too long to have you to risk so much as an eyelash of yours, ever." He kissed her lips so softly, she wasn't even sure she'd been kissed. "I know you'd like to get out of your spanking, and especially since it's going to be conducted in the great outdoors, but I really do feel that we're perfectly safe here. And if some hearty soul such as ourselves should decide to come down here, we'll see them coming and be able to compensate long before they get here."

He'd already carefully rearranged her over the car again before he'd ended his speech. "Now, you can keep a lookout as well as I can if you want. And if someone interrupts us, whether you've gotten one swat or a hundred—"

"A hundred?" she squeaked indignantly.

"—then we'll stop, and that'll be that."

"All right," Cat said, however grudgingly, realizing he hadn't asked for her acquiescence on the matter. He'd simply deemed it to be fact and plowed on.

Until now, she'd retained her jeans and panties, but she lost them just before he began, or she would have protested much more vehemently. The spanking began immediately after her jeans hit the pebbles, and the lecture began in the same instant. She wasn't sure which she disliked more.

"I know you're new to obeying me, Catherine, but I expect you to do so, the first day a rule is in effect as well as the last."

Was he spanking her harder than he had, or did it just seem louder—and worse—because they were in such an open area, where the sound reverberated across the water? She tried to keep her eyes concentrated on the road in, but it was hard when she was being compelled to dance, ankles bound by her jeans and undies, on the crunchy gravel.

She knew he wasn't hitting her as hard as he could—far from it. If he really wanted to damage her, he could do so without trying very hard, as Clint could have. But he certainly made what he did do sting and burn and ache enough that she never wanted it to happen again, most especially in this setting. So much so that her right hand began creeping backward to try to block some of the wickedly accurate, crisp swats.

"Keep your hands out in front of you, Catherine Angelique, or I'll have to take my belt off," he warned without missing a beat.

Without thinking, she fairly shrieked, "No!" then looked around as if she expected a hoard of Islanders to come to her rescue as she obediently put her hands out in front of her, where he considered they belonged. But none did, dammit. So much for those hopes.

And it wasn't just the pain of the spanking itself, it was the entirety of the action—the rules, the consequences, the lecture, the looks, the fact that someone bothered with any of them and followed them through to their conclusion, however unhappy for her.

She needed this. Every bit of it, and Finn seemed to understand that, at least as well as Clint had. He wasn't letting her get away with anything, which was exactly as she needed it to be. So few men understood that concept, really understood it and took it to heart.

Damn it.

How had she ended up with two of them in her life?

"No, ow—Finn!" He'd painted her entire backside with a primer of 'I'm sorry pink', and now he was adding another coat, just for good measure, and blast it all, that hurt!

But he kept right on spanking, and no one was riding to her rescue. He gave her a very thorough spanking that had her bawling outright near the end, and he spanked her a while beyond that so she would remember it the next time she thought about disobeying him.

But when it was done, it was done, and he took her, bare bottom into his arms, shielding her again, as he had before, from any potentially prying eyes. He rocked her tight against him, leaning up against the car and letting her stretch, unable to keep his hands from wandering down to the butt he'd just blistered.

"Ow, stop that!" She tried to swat him away, but he ignored her.

"Sorry, ma'am, but I'm a Backside Boy."

Cat groaned. He was a Backside Boy in more ways than one. He'd been born and raised on the backside of the Island, which automatically made him a Backside Boy, but he also had an affinity for roasting women's rears, which was another, deeper, some would say more twisted, reason for that particular moniker.

She shivered, and he noticed it immediately and helped her pull her clothes back on, careful around her sore butt. Then he helped her into the car, where he cranked up the heat and got them underway, eying her closely and adjusting the temperature to how he saw her acting until they were back at her house. He bundled her into bed with him and made love to her, almost painfully slowly, until she broke down in his arms and begged him to stop.

"I feel the same way, honey. I do," he confessed gruffly in the darkness.

She let him go that Monday morning, knowing that he was going to be telling his mother about them some time shortly and expecting an angry call anytime from Jane, telling her to kiss off —and much worse. Cat figured she'd be excommunicated from all of their organizations and clubs. Not that she was quite that much of a social butterfly—but still—and she'd become a social pariah. Jane's family had been on the Island a lot longer than hers had. She could do that if she wanted to. She had the power.

When it came, it wasn't as bad as she thought it was going to be. It was awkward, yes, but not nearly as horrid as she'd conjured in her mind. Still, when she saw Jane's number on the caller ID, she had more than half a mind to ignore it, but she decided to be good and pick it up anyway.

No "hello," no "how're you doing," just, "So, am I persona non grata?" she asked, fearing the answer like someone who was asking a doctor whether or not they have a terminal disease.

There was a few seconds of silence on the other end that had her heart lodging painfully in her throat, but then, "No, you're not. He's… he's the happiest I've ever seen him, and he told me he'd been waiting for you his entire life. How can I deny him that, even if thinking of it gives me the creeps?"

"I promise never to make you think of it." Cat was trying, unsuccessfully, to fight back the tears.

There was a knock at the door that she'd all but decided to ignore, but then it became an insistent pounding and she knew who it was.

"I think your son is here."

"Yeah, he told me he was going to come be with you, that he knew it was going to be hard for you to talk to me because you didn't want to hurt me."

"Of course, I didn't want to hurt you." Cat took an ineffectual swipe at the tears that were rolling down her cheeks as she made her way blindly to the foyer to let him in. "How did you ever raise a kid like that, anyway?" The half insult was taken right in stride.

"Dumb luck. Pure, dumb luck." Cat heard Jane clear her throat and knew she was crying, too.

"Thanks, Jane. I love you."

"I love you too, but if you hurt him, I'll kill you dead."

"Understood."

The phone went dead just about the time she finally got the door open, and she fell into Finn's waiting arms. He kissed her on the top of the head and carried her up the stairs as she sobbed.

"She loves the both of us very much, and she just wants us to be happy." *And have babies*, he added in his head, but he'd told her that was probably not going to happen. Jane knew that as soon as he'd told her the woman he'd been dating was Catherine. She knew that Cat didn't want kids, so she'd have to borrow grandchildren from her friends, which could have its advantages, Finn had pointed out, since she could return them when they grew annoying, and their real grandparents couldn't.

Although Jane accepted the fact that Cat was dating Finn, not everyone in their social circle was quite that accepting, as Cat found out a month or so later at the next girls' night. It was being hosted at Carol's magnificent mansion in Otter Cove. Cat arrived early, as she always did when Carol was hostessing, because despite the fact that she had all the money in the world, Carol never bothered to have these little shindigs of theirs catered, nor did she deign to get her own hands dirty, or even stop by the store for a couple of bags of chips, heaven forbid. So Cat cooked everything for her and brought it over. Everyone thought Carol was taking advantage of Cat, including Cat herself, but she liked to cook and it was no bother to her, so she'd never said or done anything about it.

Finn had been ready to give Carol a piece of his mind when she was up until all hours baking, but Cat had told him to shut up, that the menu was entirely her choice, and that Carol left things entirely up to her. And since she didn't care, there was no reason for anyone to get up in arms about it.

Finn had, of course, taken exception at being told to shut up, especially by his woman. He didn't like that at all, saying it sounded very disrespectful to his ears, and his were the ears she needed to worry about.

So, while she was literally elbow deep in flour, making a knock off of Auntie Anne's pretzels that she'd bake at Carol's tomorrow, Finn came into the kitchen, picked up a flat wooden spoon from one of the decorative utensil jugs she had scattered around the counters, and gave her bottom five very hard smacks with it. She could do very little about it without scattering flour from hell to breakfast all over her otherwise very clean kitchen. She knew that he knew she wasn't about to do that. Blast! Sometimes being a neatnik was such a pain— quite literally, this time, dammit!

"Do you know why you're getting swatted, Catherine Angelique?" he asked, giving her another hard round of five.

"Ow, ow, ow! 'Cause I told you to shut up," she said, knowing it hadn't been a good idea at the time, but she hadn't really been concentrating on him, and she was frankly sick of everyone hounding her about what she did for Carol. She wasn't as much of an idiot as everyone seemed to think she was. If she hadn't wanted to cook for Carol, she would have told her to kiss off and make her own damned food. Cooking an extra night every month gave her something enjoyable to do. She wished everyone would just back off about it, and Finn just happened to catch the brunt of it.

Unfortunately, he was the one person in her world who could also wield a wicked wooden spoon against her bottom when she mouthed off, and that was exactly what he was proceeding to do.

Chapter 10

All of the yelping and yeowling she was doing was a side effect of him smacking her with that godawful implement. She could never say how much she hated the idea of her beloved kitchen being, again, sullied by containing literally dozens of potential implements, especially when it had been safe for the past five years. He was swatting her over her jeans, in implacable sets of five or so, while chastising her about being more respectful and watching her tone of voice. Then he took them down, along with her panties.

As much as she wanted to protest the move, loudly, as she ran for any kind of cover she could, Cat had to admit that he was right. If he had told her to shut up in the same way she had said it to him, she would have been very upset. It was horrible to realize, in the middle of a spanking, how much she truly deserved it.

When he finally let her up, she could see the pattern the distinct droplets her own tears had made in the flour on the countertop before he turned her around and hugged her. He was at least as big a believer in forgiveness afterward as Clint was, which meant that she was always hugged and cuddled and completely forgiven afterward, and that was not just lip service. Unless she repeated it, she never heard about a transgression again. It was done and over with.

But she stopped him before he got to that point, saying quietly through her own tears, "I'm very sorry I said what I said. Sometimes stuff comes out of my mouth in a way I don't really intend, but that's no excuse. I didn't mean to be disrespectful of you. Thank you for correcting me."

Finn's face was, at first, wholly amazed, then it melted into adoration. "Aw, baby, that's okay. I just wanted you to be aware of what you'd said and how you'd said it. All is forgiven." He kissed her on the top of her head, but didn't—literally couldn't—stop there.

Disciplining her was an incredible aphrodisiac to him. Not just the actual act, though, but simply being responsible for her discipline and care. Watching out for her, even in the smallest of ways, making sure she was safe, protecting her, loving her—all of it kept him rock hard, twenty-four seven. Sometimes he worried that he'd overwhelm her with his attention and love, but she seemed to be reacting in the opposite manner. She was eating much better than she had, more nutritiously and more often, and she'd gained some weight. Not quite enough for his taste, but some, and he would make sure that she made steady gains in that area.

She just seemed to be happier than she had been when he first saw her again. That could definitely be ego talking. He'd even asked his mother, who had grimaced at first, not really wanting to talk about that subject with him. But then, a few days later, she had come to him and told him that yes, Cat was definitely acting much happier than she had since she'd lost her husband. It was one of the nicest compliments he'd ever received. It was better than making his first million, by a long shot.

Now, here she was, the woman of his dreams, standing there naked from the waist down, bare red bottom pressed up against the cupboards, flour covered hands and arms outstretched so they wouldn't soil anything around her, essentially unable to touch anything or move anywhere... whatever was he going to do with her?

She got to Carol's place much later than she had intended, although that still ended up being a lot earlier than any of the other girls would arrive, thankfully. At least she wouldn't have to worry they would see how flushed her face still was or how gingerly she sat down. Damn, Finn was insatiable! Not that she was really complaining, but she wasn't sure she could continue to keep up with him. She was past her sexual peak—not that her body seemed to know that—and apparently, no one had told him that he was supposed to have been, too!

He'd taken distinct advantage of the fact that she was hampered in a couple of different ways, trapped by her pants around her ankles and unable to touch anything. It was kind of strange to be half naked in her kitchen, she had to admit, but he'd wasted no time in rectifying that situation and making her completely naked, tossing her T-shirt and bra onto the floor, then leaning down to—she thought—take the rest of her clothes away from her. But he merely tightened them somehow around her feet.

"Move my jeans," she pouted, trying to dance out of them with no success.

"I don't think so," he murmured against her mouth. "I like you tethered right where you are for the time being."

His hands roamed over her body at will, tweaking here, pinching there, cupping and claiming. She couldn't part her legs very well, but that was okay with him. He slipped his middle finger into that warm ridge and found it even warmer than he'd imagined, slick with her honey, ready and waiting for him.

"I love the way a spanking always makes you wet, Catherine," he whispered, biting her nipple as she arched into his mouth.

"Does not!"

Finn chuckled. "You know better than to lie to me." He felt her contract against his finger at those words and knew he'd hit on something that was very powerful to her. "I can feel the evidence every time, like right now. You're positively drenched, and there's nothing you can do to control that. It's your body's reaction to me disciplining you."

Cat couldn't say a word. She wouldn't have said anything even if she weren't absolutely mindless from the way his finger was flicking incessantly, over and over the most sensitive spot on her body. She couldn't possibly grace his suppositions with an answer. He knew entirely too much already.

But he wouldn't allow her to come to completion. Not yet. Instead, he teased and pulled and licked and twirled and pinched, driving her absolutely crazy, but with the strict rule that she was not to let herself go until she had his permission to do so, and he was withholding that permission, forever, it seemed to Cat.

But not forever, because, eventually, he leaned down and freed her feet, then took a step back from her and adjusted his own jeans. He didn't take them off but only loosed himself, so that she was still entirely nude and slightly hampered, and he was fully dressed.

He gathered her legs up and over his arms and entered her all at once, then planted his hands on the counter next to her, saying gutturally, "Hold on tight. You're going to need to," not caring that his shirt would wear her floury handprints until the next time he washed it.

And she did. It was a wild, uncontrolled ride that threw her into orgasm after orgasm, nonstop the entire time.

It was no wonder she was still flushed and a little sweaty—even after their shower—when she arrived on Carol's doorstep. The kitchen door was always open—and if it wasn't, she knew where the key was hidden—and she made it in, loaded down with bags and trays, in only one trip.

She was surprised to find Carol waiting for her at the small breakfast table. Her husband had divorced her several years ago, and as her kids were grown, she'd had less and less to do and more and more time to drink. "You're late," she said, and Cat could tell she'd been drinking even before she saw the tumbler full of what she knew was whiskey, neat, on the table in front of her, and the half gallon of JW, half empty, next to it.

Cat put her coat over the other chair and turned to her food. "I'm a little later than usual, but then, I do this on my own time, so there's no real schedule."

"Were you busy banging your new boyfriend?" Carol sneered.

So it's going to be that way, Cat thought. She'd known things had gone a little too easy. She took a deep breath and turned, facing her friend. "As a matter of fact, yes, I was."

"If I'da known that my friendsh kids were fair game, I'd've gone after him myshelf," she slurred, hoisting her drink for another gulp. Carol had never sipped a drink in her life. She had no grasp of the concept whatsoever.

"Well, actually, Finn pursued me, not the other way around. Not that it's any of your business."

Carol was not to be placated. "That still doesn't make it right, to just up and fuck the son of a woman who's been your best friend all your life! You watched him grow up, for God's sake! Do you realize that when we were in college, he was in grade school? That's just sick!"

Cat resolutely began to repack the things she'd just taken out, piling them neatly by the door so that she could make it back out to her car in one trip.

"Where're you goin'?" Carol asked, draining her drink in one last, big gulp. "Home to screw him again?"

Cat had had just about enough. She walked toward Carol, who leaned back a little in her chair and tried to focus, without much success, apparently. "People in glass bottles shouldn't throw stones." Cat picked up the bottle of whiskey and emptied it into the waiting tumbler. "Have another glass, Carol. I'm going home to my drop dead gorgeous, thirty-five year old billionaire boyfriend who's hung like a horse, fucks me satyr and thinks the sun rises and sets on me." She pushed the full glass in front of her former friend. "So, how's Johnny Walker working out for you as a lover, hmmm?"

She turned and walked calmly out, loaded down like a pack mule and pissed as hell, and she jumped five miles into the air when she heard something glass hit the door behind her. Carol had either thrown the glass or the bottle. Cat was betting on the bottle, since that was the one that was empty.

She held it together until she got home, but her hands were shaking as she put her key into the lock. She'd lied to Carol; Finn wasn't home. In fact, he'd left for Boston on business again, and wouldn't be home for several days, so there was no one home to comfort her. But old habits die hard, and before she could truly collapse, she put everything—and that meant everything, down to the last stick of butter—back in its rightful place.

The phone had rung several times while she busied herself not thinking about what had just happened, but she'd already turned off the answering machine first thing in the door. She really didn't want to talk to anyone, not even Finn. Hell, not even Clint, if he were here. But then, if he was here, this situation would never have come about.

When all of the stuff she'd carted over to Carol's and back had been put away, she'd cleaned the oven, then the fridge, and now she was washing down the cabinets. When the neatniks get upset, they clean. If she was really upset, she'd tackle the attic next.

It was nearly six, about the time when Jane, who was the next earliest, would have arrived at Carol's to help Cat out with whatever she needed, and the phone began ringing incessantly, as if the caller was quite sure she was home, just not answering. She should have taken it off the hook, but the neurotic side of her just couldn't. She glanced at the caller ID, already knowing who it was and that she was probably in big trouble.

"Hello." She couldn't even work up a good cry. He was going to think everything was hunky dory with her and that she was playing some kind of game or something.

"I'm on my way home now. The plane lands in Bangor in thirty minutes, and I'll be home in an hour or so. Are you all right?"

"Home? But you have work—"

"Work can wait. Don't you know that you're the most important thing on this earth to me?"

That brought on the waterworks. "But how did you know?"

"Mom went over to Carol's not long ago and she confessed everything. She was downright suicidal, so Mom's staying with her, or you know she would be there with you in a heartbeat. We've both been trying to get ahold of you for the past few hours, but someone hasn't been answering her phone," he said pointedly. Which is a subject about which they would speak when he got home, but he didn't want to upset her any further by saying that, so he kept it to himself.

She hiccoughed, "I've been c-cleaning."

The soft, reassuring tone of his voice was almost worse

than if he had sounded angry with her for being incommunicado. "I figured as much. I want you to answer the phone when it rings from now on, if you recognize the number and it's Mom or myself, Catherine. Understand? You don't have to talk to anyone else right now but us, but you do have to talk to us."

Cat was literally bawling. "Y-yes."

"Good girl. Now go lie down, but keep the phone where you can get to it. I bet Mom'll call you shortly, and she's very worried about you."

"I will."

"Sleep if you can. Everything will be fine, I promise, honey."

"Okay."

Finn's heart clenched in his chest at how tiny and afraid she sounded. Cat might have been physically small, but she rarely sounded it. He knew he shouldn't have let himself be talked into going on this stupid Boston trip. Next time, he'd listen to his gut instinct. It hadn't led him wrong yet. He could easily have foregone this trip, but he'd listened to someone who'd encouraged him to go to make contacts on the east coast. He didn't need contacts there. He had more than enough money to support himself and Cat quite regularly for the rest of their lives.

He'd said he was going to retire once he came back to the Island, yet he kept letting his love of the business drag him away from the woman he loved. Well, no more. He was going to concentrate and dedicate his life to her. Finn allowed himself a small smile. He wasn't quite sure whether Cat was going to be happy about that or not, considering it was probably going to mean that her backside was going to be roasted a lot more frequently than it would if he continued to let himself be pulled in a thousand different directions.

But he also knew that she would benefit from such close attention, as would their relationship. He opened his briefcase for a moment and looked at the velvet box hidden there. Inside, was a stunning five-carat diamond ring, with which he intended to propose to Cat. He knew it was still early, some might say too early, in their relationship. But he took all of the lessons he'd learned from Clint to heart, most especially the last one—none of us knows how long we have on this planet. And he intended to spend as much of it as he could, married, bound any and every possible way, to his Catherine. If he thought he could get away with it, he'd chain her to him, although he realized the impracticalities of that arrangement. Still, it had its advantages.

He'd thought about asking her to move into a new house with him and live with him for a while. But he thought that would really just be a stopgap measure. He wanted her to be his wife, not just his housemate and lover. Finn knew there were going to be issues around it for her—landmine issues about abandoning Clint and the house, and he'd do whatever he could to accommodate her. They could keep the house and she could go to it anytime she wanted. They'd keep it forever if she wanted to. He would let her decide if and when she wanted to part with it. It would be entirely her decision, and he would not be jealous of a house when she was in his bed every night and over his lap when he deemed necessary.

Once he landed and claimed his baggage and retrieved his car, he drove like a maniac over route 1A, pothole hell that it was in spring, praying there were no cops. He knew the road so well from having driven it while he was growing up on the Island that he could pretty much do it on autopilot.

When he pulled up to her house, it was dark and quiet, although she'd left the light on for him. He used the key she'd given him a few weeks ago, sick of having to get up to let him in when he arrived in the middle of the night.

As usual, as quiet as he tried to be, she awoke as soon as he entered the room, sitting up in the middle of the big bed.

"I'm sorry you had to come back, but I'm glad you did." Cat held her arms out to him, and he dropped everything—suitcase, garment bag, computer bag, everything, right where he was—and launched himself toward her, grabbing her up in a big bear hug and just rocking and holding her tight, stroking her hair and patting her back.

"I'm so sorry you had to go through something like that, angel."

Cat sniffed and clung to him like he was the only solid thing in the world, and Finn's heart soared. He adored it when she opened herself up to him enough to latch onto him like this.

"It's okay. Your mom was so okay with it, someone had to give me guff about it somewhere down the line. And Carol, I can handle."

Finn took the opportunity to make them a little bit more comfortable, piling pillows against the headboard then gathering her back into his bear hug arms. "I understand from Mom that you gave her quite the dressing down, and that I have been elevated to the ranks of billionaire."

Cat snorted and blushed beautifully, shrugging. "I don't know what your financial situation is, of course, and there's no need to tell me, really, but judging by your car, you aren't doin' too badly. So I might have embellished a smidge, to make a point."

"I don't care whether or not you know about my finances, Cat. I want you to know everything about me. I've just been taking things slowly because I didn't want to push you. I know how much you loved Clint, and I wouldn't want to do anything that would dishonor his memory in your eyes."

She shook her head. Where in the hell had he come from, anyway, and, more than that, what could she possibly have done to deserve him? She already knew the answer to the second question was absolutely nothing, especially since he was the second time she'd found someone who was perfect for her.

Somewhere down the line, there was going to be some serious reckoning happening on her account. The karmic books were seriously lopsided in her favor, although she knew that he was going to do his level best to balance the books with his palm across her bottom on a regular basis. But for now, she was going to let go and enjoy what she was lucky enough to have, and so she snuggled down into his arms, content just to let him hold her.

When he popped the question, several months later, it was right after he'd given her a thorough blistering for not calling him to tell him she was going to be late home from going out to dinner with his mother. He'd asked her to be home by ten, which he thought was more than reasonable, considering they'd left at six.

But he should have remembered how she and his mom could—and would—talk and reminded her about her rule to call him if she was going to be late, although he also reminded her that he shouldn't have to remind her of her rules.

Of all the rules he made for her, which really weren't too many, it was the ones that restricted her freedom, as far as she was concerned, that she chafed against the most and therefore were the most likely to ignored.

So he was quite ready for her to blow off the call he should have received some time before ten. But then it got to be eleven. And twelve. And then one. Cell reception was notoriously bad on the Island, and he wasn't getting through to either of them. But there were pockets of reception on the plan he'd switched her over to, and she was expected to find one and make at least one call to let him know she was okay and ask—and he meant ask—if she could come home later.

None of that was done, and he was getting a little frantic. He made a mental note to switch his mom over to the same plan Cat was on, if only for his own mental health.

They dragged themselves in at about 1:30 by taxi. All the way from Bangor, but considering their condition, he was glad they had, and he personally paid their tab and gave the guy a healthy tip. He'd never seen his mom quite so polluted. She was teetering on her high heels and just about knocked him over with the alcohol on her breath when she went to hug him.

Catherine wasn't in much better condition, either, but she was a quieter drunk. She merely stood there, staring at him, bleary eyed, with a strange grin on her face. He couldn't tell if she was happy or getting ready to ralph.

He got his mom tucked away into one of the guest rooms well away from the master bedroom, although he wasn't really worried that she was going to hear anything, because as soon as she hit the bed, fully clothed, she passed out, thankfully.

Cat was right where he'd left her. Hadn't moved a muscle as far as he could tell. Finn stood directly in front of her. "Are you all right?"

She nodded, smiling that eerily beatific smile at him.

"You know you're in trouble, don't you?"

More happy nodding. "For not calling you. But I din't have no sing-signal."

"You're going to get a signal, believe me, woman." He took her hand, made her step out of her killer spike heels before she killed herself, then brought her out onto the deck instead of the bedroom. It was a warm, early summer night, just perfect for correcting ladies who got drunk and forgot the rules made to keep them safe and protected.

She was wearing that pink dress, the one she'd worn on their first date. It had him salivating, wanting to bend her over the railing for an entirely different purpose, but he steeled himself in his resolve and made her ready.

The first connection of the flat of his hand with her rounded cheeks had her considerably more sober than she cared to be in that situation. Cat suddenly realized where she was and what was just beginning to happen. "Finn! No!"

"Oh, yes, my love. I've been frantic about the two of you all night. It's time you felt a little frantic yourself."

And she did, more than a little, as he built the heat in her bottom to blazing proportions, ignoring her pleas for mercy and the inevitable tears, which he hated to see but which he didn't allow to deter him from applying the necessary amount of correction to her glowing rear end.

He stopped at one point, although he wasn't done, to reach into his pants pocket. "I was going to give this to you tonight when you got home, but somehow I think it's even more appropriate to give it to you in this position, and I think I'll like the answer better if you're a bit tipsy when you give it."

Finn kept her bent over, but got down on one knee anyway, and showed her the ring. She would have moved toward him, but his hand stayed her. "Catherine Angelique, I would be so honored if you would do me the honor of becoming my wife."

She was crying again, but not for the same reason as she was before. She was overwhelmed and could only say, "Yes!"

He slipped the ring onto her finger quickly, as if he thought she might reconsider, then he stood and snicked his belt out of his pants. Finn heard her quickly indrawn breath at the sound. "I'll hug you when we're done, but we're not quite finished here, my love."

That thick black belt lashed across the crest of those generous hillocks, making her dance even more fervently than had his hand.

Finn stepped forward to examine his handiwork in the pale moonlight. "That's gonna leave a mark. I hope."

The End

Carolyn Faulkner

The words "spanking" and "discipline" have always sent a shiver up Carolyn Faulkner's spine. She knows she's not alone. Writing started as a way to explore her feelings. Soon short stories flowed from her pen featuring reluctant heroes taking the leading lady in hand, but always for her own good.

Today Carolyn is the author of dozens of books. She writes from her home in Maine, where she lives with her husband and leading man.

You can read an interview with Carolyn here:
http://www.blushingbooks.com/blog/?p=175

You may check out her website while it's under construction here:
http://www.carolynfaulkner.com

Don't miss these exciting titles by Carolyn Faulkner and Blushing Books!

Series books
Gentle Series
Her Gentle Giant
Her Gentle Cowboy
Her Gentle Soldier
Her Gentle Gangster

The Alpha's Woman series
The Alpha's Woman

Single Titles
Old enough to Know Better
Maddie and Daddy
Transgressions
The Brothers Rule
The Eye of the Beholder
Made to Order Bride
His Sugarbaby
Mr. Sunshine
No, Sir
His Runaway Bride
Undercover Sir
The Lark and The Bull
Doctor's Orders
A Babygirl for Christmas
Her Handyman
The Hart of the Matter
At His Hand
King of Hearts
True Desires
Lord Belden's Baggage
In His Care
Correct Me If I'm Wrong
Beauty Of The Beast
Tamed To His Hand
Daddy!
Amanda and the Stable Master
Lion
The Banished King
Northern Belle
The Cherished One
Forever Wife
Grace's Demon
Beauty's Beast

Blushing Books

Blushing Books is the oldest eBook publisher on the web. We've been running websites that publish steamy romance and erotica since 1999, and we have been selling eBooks since 2003. We have free and promotional offerings that change weekly, so please do visit us at http://www.blushingbooks.com/free.

Blushing Books Newsletter

Please join the Blushing Books newsletter
to receive updates & special promotional offers.
You can also join by using your mobile phone:
Just text **BLUSHING** to 22828.

Every month, one new sign up via text messaging will receive
a $25.00 Amazon gift card, so sign up today!